PAREIDOLIA

Pareidolia

Edited by
James Everington
& Dan Howarth

BLACK
SHUCK
BOOKS

First published in Great Britain in 2019 by
Black Shuck Books
Kent, UK

Into the Wood

Sarah Read

*

I don't know whether it was Thea who changed the house or the house who changed Thea, but I noticed the house first. The way the woodgrain noticed us back – a thousand faces staring out from narrow panels that warped away from the cabin walls. And when the wind slammed the side of the house, the place would rock and rock and rock and boards would bob and nod. *Yes*, they said, *yes yes yes.* Though I hadn't been aware of asking any questions. Not at the time.

Thea stared, eyes wide as those wooden whorls, and nodded along. *Yes*, she nodded, "yes," she whispered. Her eyes as dead as the dark spots on the wood that looked more like faces to me than any face I'd ever seen. You wouldn't have blamed me for thinking it was all a game. She was an odd child. Not quite odd enough to put me off her daddy, but odd enough that plenty before me had been. Brian says it's my compassion that keeps me with them both, but he's never been on the streets. I can tolerate an odd teen. I can tolerate walls that stare back at me so long as those walls keep the warm in.

Desperation, I guess, looks a lot like compassion. Resignation looks like patience. You could say I gave an inch. Didn't know then how much a house could take. It's been too long since I've known a house at all.

There was a house. One that my mother ruled. My mother always loved birds best, which is why she called me after one, and why she kept me like one. My name is Cassidy Diana Dee. Cassi-dee-dee-dee, like the birds outside my window sang – the birds outside the cage.

Father flew when I was young, as soon as he knew that I would never know him, never see him for his face. He was always changing his coat, his beard – to me, he was never the same man twice. Always a stranger coming through the door, always a threat. I screamed every time I saw him, and eventually he stopped coming through the door altogether. Mama never forgave me. But Mama always wore the same coat, and the same broken expression – the twist of her mouth so familiar, I could almost recognize her, almost.

I fell from that nest before I could fly – landed in the dirt with the worms. I don't like to be touched, but a girl can make a living on the phone. Facsimile touch. A bird in the dirt can glut herself on worms, if she digs. And in the forest of city buildings, every tree has an abandoned nest. Somewhere to roost, if you can stand the cold.

I can't remember faces, not even dangerous ones, not even my own. But I know voices. The way a bird can recognize signals in song. I can tell Landon from Justin on the phone, remember what they like – how to keep them on the line or get them off quick if another call is coming in.

I'd set up someplace warm, where I could take my calls in peace. Trevor's Tavern was best, where the man behind the bar was always Trevor, or at least always answered to the name. Where my face was as anonymous as everyone else's was to me. And when the phone was quiet, sometimes the drinks were free.

When I saw Brian come through the door of Trevor's, I knew he'd have a place, somewhere warm in the world. His coat was worn in a way that told me it was his only one; beard so long I knew he never trimmed it. I watched from the bar as I wrapped up my call, counting as the minutes on my burner phone ticked down. He sat, alone, with his hands as scruffed as old gloves wrapped around a big stack of keys. When he put his down coat around my shoulders at the end of the evening, I could feel their weight in the pocket against my hip, like a promise that there were sturdy doors to get behind. Heavy like an anchor, keeping me from flying away. It was his only coat, he said. I could always know him by it.

He told me about little Thea that night, before he even told me his whole name. The honest sort. I could probably have told him then that I had nowhere to go, but I didn't want to risk it. Nests with fledglings are often the most comfortable and I'd been sleeping rough for weeks.

So instead I danced – we danced. I tolerated the touch and I told him with my body that I wanted to go with him. We drove out of the city, into the woods, to his log cabin. His nest.

The cabin was a bramble of stacked trees, the bark still clinging in flyaway curls to the outside. Inside, a deep and dirty carpet grabbed at my feet. The walls were lined with thin pressboard panels that pulled away from their glue and tacks as the house shifted and aged. A threadbare velvet sofa sagged in front of a television, and on it perched a girl with braids in her hair, her hands over her face as she peered at cartoons through her fingers.

I suspected Thea had been a deal-breaker for him in the past – that her name became a filter I had slipped through. A test I had passed. By the end of the week, when he wondered where else I was supposed to be, he was more than happy with my answer: "right here." I've never had any experience running a home. No nest management. Never had any good examples, either, but I've seen them on TV.

The teens on TV want expensive phones, clothes. They want to stay out late, to fly solo. Thea wanted these things, too, but had to settle for less. Brian had gotten her the phone, scavenged the clothes, but friends to stay out with are harder to find, if you're odd. I've always been good at working with less. I could do that, be a companion for her. What I couldn't do was sit and watch her bob her head in time with the nodding walls, when the wind kicked up and the walls shifted and the boards danced. Or hold her gaze when she turned, and her eyes were as flat as wood, skin grained with whorls and knots. The curls that Brian would braid and re-braid hanging in a tangle like Spanish moss from a winter tree. I couldn't stop her from standing or hold her back from the door. I couldn't touch the dry roughness of her skin.

And I couldn't bring myself to follow her when she walked from the cabin, out into the bending and whipping trees, shaking their branches *no no no*.

I couldn't see her through the dark, through the storm. And I couldn't call Brian. The wind had knocked the trees into the lines. All was down and my burner phone had ticked all the way to empty. I could only wait in the dark and listen to the house. Learn its voice, learn its song. No light. No phones. Only the wind and me whispering "she's gone" and the house answering *yes yes yes*.

But I'm still here?

Yes yes yes.

❄

Storms here seal you up against the edge of the wood and no light gets in. Not like the always-bright of the city. Brian came home early, but the dark made it seem late. It was too late, anyway.

"Thea! Thea! Thea!" He called all around the house, but the wind had blown over and the boards said nothing. Stillness. He found me staring out the back window, like an owl watching a bird feeder.

"Cass, where's Thea?"

"She went out."

"You let her go out in that storm? Where? Who with?"

He was mad. Was this our first fight? Our last? Would I sleep in the woods that night? Would Thea?

The boards were still.

"She just...left. I couldn't stop her."

"Who with?"

"No one! She just walked out." *I think the walls told her to.* Maybe Thea had been the one asking questions all along.

He ran to the phone. Picked it up, slammed it down. It would be a while before the lines were repaired and before the lights came on. Nothing happens quickly in the woods.

"Which way did she walk?"

I pointed to the line of swaying trees.

He swore. I hadn't heard him do that before – that was a new note to his song, and he started for the trees.

"Stay here in case she comes back" he called back to me.

I nodded. *Yes yes yes,* and the house nodded with me.

I sat in the living room and met each pair of grainy eyes in the walls till I found her. Undeniably Thea. The curve of her face there in the grain. A burred rent for a mouth. A face I hadn't seen there before – a face I would not have recognized if I'd seen it a thousand times in the flesh – right there in the wall, nodding more softly than the others. A face I saw and knew, here in her home.

Brian carried Thea out of the woods in his arms, as he must have carried her as a child. Her head bobbed against the crook of his arm as he crossed the weedy patch of meadow behind the trailer. He laid her on the couch, not far from her face in the wall – and that panel seemed to twist, to crane – to see what had become of her.

Her skin was raked with rashes. Striped and whorled. Her fingers twisted into knots and unfurled like roots searching for soft earth. I brought her water and she drank, and even the water that she spilled seemed to soak in. Brian rushed between her and the bathroom where I could hear a tub filling. Could smell the clean steam. I wanted to crawl into that hot water and wash away the feeling of all those eyes on me, but it wasn't my bath. Not even my bathroom.

"Help me," Brian said.

We peeled off her damp clothes and clumps of soil fell to the carpet and disappeared into its pile. We carried her to the bathroom and placed her in that sudsy water. The rash had spread to the skin beneath her clothes. Her eyes were fixed wide, roving. Her skin hard and rough. She didn't even sigh when the warm water closed over her. She just lay in it. She said nothing. Brian whimpered.

The walls leaned in. The burred throat of Thea's wooden face twisted wider.

He took her to the hospital but left her face here in the wood with me.

I had the house to myself.

I took that bath. I took a nap. I took my time. I took and I took and it felt more like home by the hour.

I walked softly so the boards wouldn't sway. Only their eyes moved, tracing me into the lines of house.

I pinned a pillowcase over Thea's face. Didn't want to feel those eyes on me, following me, or see that twisting mouth. If I pressed my ear up against that sheet, to the place where the sharp edges of the wood split, I could hear her. Sigh or wind. Scream or gale. I never mistake a voice. But all she could say anymore was "yes" because that was how she was tacked down.

Tacked to the house like a specimen in a case. My heart pinched for her, then.

I took pliers from the case under the eaves. It was hard to find the small dark pins in that maze of woodgrain, but I found them and I pulled and pulled till the board came away. There was filthy paper and plaster and mildew behind where it had been pressed to the wall. Brown flecks of dried glue and the watermarks of the house's own perspiration. The fine veneer was adhered to a sheet of old vinyl as yellowed and brittle as old taffy.

I washed the board in the bath, cleaned away the dust and debris. Smoothed out the splinters. Let the dry panel soak life-giving water deep into its processed pulp. I tucked the board into Thea's bed, but still the whorl eyes gaped.

I pulled the blanket over that wooden face and something heavy fell from the folds of the quilt. Her phone. Not like my burner, but bright, endless.

With the landlines down and my phone on empty, I couldn't work. No Landon or Justin – no income. My nest egg diminishing. But these expensive phones, they have ways of working when other things don't. I could work from anywhere, with this. Anytime. I navigated to my profile and updated the number to Thea's. And I was back to work in minutes, sighing, cooing, facsimile affection.

I wondered what the faces on the walls saw – the sounds of a show with no pictures, no images, just as they are only pictures that make no sound. The way I see faces, when they aren't the wooden kind.

※

The keys let someone in the door – it must be Brian – and I squeezed my eyes shut until he murmured for me, and I knew his voice.

I squeezed the button that sent Thea's phone to sleep, to silence, and its black screen gaped like the open wooden mouths.

He moved like a ghost through the house, pulling a bag from the closet and filling it with Thea's clothes. He didn't see the board tucked under the blanket, didn't see the face of his daughter frozen there in a silent scream. He didn't notice the one board missing from the peeling walls. The other faces nodded on and on as he walked back and forth, creating drafts, compressing the floor and letting it up again and setting all those loose faces in motion. I wondered if there were more faces beneath his feet. Under the carpet. Their open mouths pressed against our soles, trying to chew their way through.

He shook his stack of keys free from his pocket. He told me to make myself comfortable, to make myself at home. I promised I would. I said it standing in his kitchen, in his slippers, with the taste of his coffee coating my tongue. He asked me to watch the house. Though this house can watch itself.

He left again.

I made myself a meal, made a mess, made myself at home. Made myself *a* home. I watched the house and the house watched me.

※

Brian was back again in the night. I stirred from my nest of blankets on the couch. It was dark, the lights still off, but I knew him by his breathing, by the tension in his inhale.

"Cass?"

"I'm here."

"Help me with her. Help me get her into bed."

I raced to her room and slipped her face beneath her pillow, the thin wood fibers still soft with wet. I knew my running must have sent all those faces bobbing agreement, knew that they approved, but I couldn't see them in the dark. I hurried back, imagined another frantic wave of yesses, and I took some of the burden of Thea's body from Brian's arms. We folded the child into her bed, tucked the down around her, safe and warm.

Brian felt his way from furniture to furniture. Even he seemed to know not to run his fingers along the wall. He made his way to the kitchen, where he pulled a big flashlight down from the top of the fridge. I hadn't known one was there. Now I do. Soon I'll know the place for everything.

He checked the batteries and turned toward the back

door. "The doctor wants me to look in the woods around where I found her. See if she might have eaten any toxic plants."

The wind had picked up again. In the light from the flashlight, I could see the walls nodding in agreement.

Yes yes yes go into the wood.

"Will you keep an eye on Thea for me? Watch her till I get back?" I nodded, *yes yes yes.*

I perched, watching, at that same window as he disappeared, and then so did his light.

And his face watched me, over my shoulder, nodding and smiling himself away.

I lit one of the small candles on the mantle. I took another bath, another nap. Took the pliers and took Brian's face down from the wall. I bathed board Brian, his coy smile writ plain as day in the grain. I sat him in the chair by Thea's bed. He could watch her, now, always.

I pulled board Thea from beneath the pillow and I took the hammer from the case under the eaves. I gathered the old, dark pins from the corners of the carpet pile. I tacked her face back to where it should be. The pliable, wet wood shaped to her skull, to the curve of her nose and the hollow of her eyes, and the tacks held it in place. And for the first time in my life, I recognized a person there in front of me. It was her, and I'd know her when I saw her. I could see her even without her voice, written in the wood.

I stared, in awe of the convenience of recognition. And as the wood dried, it twisted, and her face twisted with it. Her, but warped. Her mouth too, too wide, her eyes not where they should be, but hers. And as he dried, board Brian curled and collapsed, with no skull to hold his shape, no body to hold him up. He twisted into a curl of himself, thin wood fibers bristling like pinfeathers.

They had no roots here, anymore, to hold them. You need to put down roots to build a home, and they had none – just drifting curls of wood silently screaming. I know that song.

I have a home now. A house. All you need to do to make a home is get inside the walls and stay out of the wood. Put down your roots. Keep the door locked and wake up to bird song, until it's time to fly again. Yes, *yes*, I'll fly again, when the nest gets brittle, as soon as I let go of this anchor of keys.

Joss Papers for Porcelain Ghosts

Eliza Chan

*

"Nothing followed you?" Harriet's mother said, peering up and down the corridor.

"No, Mum," Harriet replied. She looked pointedly at her suitcase, hair clammy around her forehead and neck. She hadn't slept in nearly twenty hours thanks to the baby next to her on the plane. "Can you let me in?"

She had to duck under the white banner draped above the doorway: the Chinese calligraphy done hastily, acknowledging death within, the spidery script dripping black ink downwards. Like raindrops on a car window, growing heavy as they merged. There had been so many long journeys in childhood.

Her mother finally nodded, ushering her in, notching the double locks behind her before she finally acknowledged her daughter. "Shoes off ah!"

Harriet was halfway to the enticing fan before shuffling back to remove her footwear. She had fallen out of the habit. Steven had been brought up in a household that only removed their shoes before bed.

"Who would be following me anyway?" she asked.

"Not who – what," her mother said over the hissing kettle from the kitchen.

Time had stood still in the last four years since Harriet had visited her por-por's flat. Or more likely, the last three decades since Gong-gong had passed away. The wall of family photos had grown slightly. She recognised her daughters, Lucy and Mia from last year's Christmas card. Next to it was her own faded school photo: face beaming under thick rimmed plastic glasses and badly cut fringe. None of Steven. It was bad enough her mother moved overseas and married a gweilo, but Harriet had gone one step further and had kids with one without even stopping to marry him first.

Harriet went to the household shrine to light her joss sticks before she got told off. The imposing mahogany unit had a carved roof like a tiered pagoda and shelves underneath filled with books and knick-knacks. Por-por had brought Guanyin with her when she came to the UK. No crucifixes and hymns needed but instead food and flowers. Egg tarts, fresh fruit, and fresh cups of tea were left daily. Today there was a pyramid of oranges, a large pineapple and flowers in a blue and white vase. She remembered that vase. Por-por had moved over when Harriet was nine and things started to go wrong for her parents. Slept in Harriet's bed, whilst she fumed on the floor, listening to the motor of an old steam train heaving in her sleep. But to make up for it, at the Chinese supermarket, her por-por had let her choose her own chopsticks and rice bowl, even pick the vase for Guanyin's flowers that her gran took back to Hong Kong nearly a year later. There were plenty of vases in China, but only one that had been handpicked by her granddaughter, she had explained. And so they had to visit, Harriet and her mother, to check in on Por-por, on the vase and on the goddess.

The statue was covered with a cloth, and Harriet was about to remove it when her mother came from the tiny kitchen with a screech. "What are you doing? Don't touch that!"

Harriet flinched like she had been slapped, her nerves shot through. Her hand jumped back and knocked the vase over. She watched it teeter on the narrow base, water slopping from the brim as if she was not even there, a spirit without any means to stop it. When it smashed on the tiled floor, Harriet felt an odd sense of relief.

"Aiyah," her mother said, crouching to pick up the shards.

"Sorry, I'm... tired I guess. But why is Guanyin covered?" Harriet said.

"It's bad luck for the gods to see leh... because of Por-por." Her mother had already cleaned it up, like there had been no mess in the first place. She snatched the joss sticks from Harriet, shaking her head as if she had been brandishing a knife. Returned to folding the heap of laundry. She held up a beige polo shirt. "How about this one for tomorrow?" her mother asked, staring past Harriet.

Harriet turned to look behind her, but it was only Por-

por's empty chair in front of the TV. Two strokes in the last year and a stubborn refusal to move into a nursing home. Her mother had flown over to Hong Kong six months ago, their roles now reversed. A phone call at one in the morning, her mother's voice robotic as she told her it was too late. Por-por had gone. No, she didn't need to come, it's fine. Harriet felt a hollow guilt in her stomach that had nothing to do with the tepid aeroplane meal or jet lag. She had been going to visit, she had always planned to. All through late primary and into high school, she and her mother visited every year. Then Harriet had wanted to try something new: a girls' holiday in Spain, a European break with a boyfriend. She was studying, she was working, she was saving... Mia happened. Lucy a year later. And Harriet never knew what to say to Por-por over the phone with her broken Cantonese. Could never find the time, putting it on the back burner along with decorating the spare bedroom and learning Spanish.

Her mother looked at her – pouring Harriet a mug of boiling hot water from a thermos – exactly what she wanted in the local humidity. She bit back her complaint, blowing until the heat steamed up her glasses and she drank it down in thirsty sips.

"I told you not to come," her mother said, the laundry now in one tidy pile. Her hands couldn't keep still. Wiping one spot on the coffee table over and over.

"It's okay. Steven's parents said they'll help. He can survive for a week," Harriet said, reaching to squeeze her mother's arm. "I wanted to be here for you."

"Hai... but there's just so much to do. Your uncles and

auntie are arriving tomorrow, we need to meet with the monk and..."

"Mum, let me help," Harriet said, "What can I do?"

Her mother patted her hand, "I don't think you will understand."

Harriet bristled with the defensive spikes of every "gweipor" snigger from shop assistants; every Chinese New Year greeting she stumbled and faltered over on the phone as a chorus of relatives lined up to correct her intonation; every look of pity when she asked for the English menu. Her arm stiffened beneath her mother's touch. "I can help," she insisted.

"Hor ah, you want to help. Look after your por-por," her mum said.

Harriet heard the laughter from next door's TV through the wall in the silence that followed. "What?" Harriet said finally. The happy jingle of an advert was playing now from the unseen TV, the low tones of the narrator droning under Harriet's skin.

Her mother pointed at the small dining table. Only then did Harriet noticed that her por-por's place was still set, chopsticks, spoon and all. Her favourite cushion was plumped up and her purple buttoned vest draped over the chairback. "We still have to look after her wor."

※

She was getting delirious with the lack of sleep. There were only two beds in the flat and these went to the elder uncles and their wives. Harriet had offered to book a hotel but no, her mother said firmly, if she was here now, she would stay with family. Space was tight and privacy lacking. She slept on the unpadded wooden bench that was her grandmother's sofa, above the ratcheting snores of her mother and auntie on an airbed below. Ornate dragon clawed handles may be beautiful to look at, but they did nothing pushed against her forehead as she tried to stretch and turn on the narrow seat. And when she woke, she found saw things in every shadow: a man at the dinner table, hunched over a bowl of soup; a woman's shoulder just visible beyond the open bedroom door; a head glaring at her from the shrine ledge.

"Haven't you seen her yet? She probably doesn't forgive you," Uncle Lei said. He had seen Por-por this morning. At five in the morning when he woke to go for tai chi in the park, he had seen her. Uncle Lei was rather pleased with himself since the others had all seen Por-por already and he was sick of being lumped with Harriet. He had been heading out of the door when he felt someone touching his shoulder like she used to do before giving him a lecture. And when he turned, he saw something, just out of the corner of his eye, for a second. Her ghost.

Auntie Pui-Ling decided it was high time to tell her story again, because she hadn't repeated it in the last three hours. She had shut the kitchen door, definitely, because of the oil smells she always shut the kitchen door, but it opened, completely by itself! That was definitely Por-por. Por-por didn't approve of spring onion pancakes when Auntie was supposedly losing weight. So they put the stack onto Por-por's plate instead and the whole family yammered encouragingly to the empty chair, telling her spirit to enjoy them whilst they were still hot.

Her mum opened the window and turned off the air conditioning because Por-por had scolded her about the waste of money. Uncle Freddie bought salted fish for dinner because of a whisper in his ear she was craving it.

It was no good talking about coincidences and delusions. Harriet had tried that, but they just shook their heads at her, sad at her disbelief. It had to be Steven. He hadn't even paid for dinner that time he came to Hong Kong and he even had the audacity to cross chopsticks with Por-por. Didn't show her any face, no respect for his elders! And living in sin with Harriet: she was in the bad books, the only logical explanation why she hadn't seen Por-por's ghost.

Harriet had to excuse herself from the dinner table, pretending to look at her phone with her back to them. She stared at a vase of flowers. The blue floral motif looked like frilly lion heads, recurring in a spotty pattern that reminded her with a pang of potato printing with her own daughters. Wondered if Steven would remember their ballet lessons and drive with the noise of insistent singalongs from the backseat. Lucy would be louder to make up for her lack of tone, glancing at her older sister and copying every mannerism she could see. Tapping out a short message, Harriet noticed something moving out of the corner of her eye.

Gwei.

She froze, resisting the urge to look. Her relatives were yammering in Cantonese, gossiping about her as if the language barrier would be enough to hide the conversation. She tried to tune out, easy enough with her limited language skills. Still she could not ignore the pointed looks her Uncle Lei threw her, the gesticulating chopsticks, that whatever she had done, they disapproved. Her mother's face was a mirror to the stern door god at the entrance of the apartment block. She spooned some fish atop Por-por's untouched white mound of rice, her silence blacker than a starless night.

Gwei ar.

This time the voices were closer. Whispers that breathed lightly on her arm like limp mosquitoes. Her eyes strained with the effort of keeping them still, calmly focused on her phone. The words she had typed blurred and migrated across the screen as if tipping out of the corner. She would not succumb to the suffocating hysteria in the room. No matter the jet lag, the migraines pushing at her temples, she was not that person.

Gwei ar, gwei ar, gwei ar.

Very slowly, she inched her eyes up from her phone. Past the bowl of oranges, the spiked stems of burnt out joss stick like needles in a pin cushion, past the screaming faces on the flower vase and up to the…

Harriet looked at the vase again. Chrysanthemum heads, that's all they were, chrysanthemum blooms. But she had smashed that vase. The one she had chosen when her parents had been screaming the house down at each other. The one her por-por had nodded at, the language of hand gestures and folding paper cranes; the chicken drumstick fresh from the chopping board for a hungry stomach; a warm hand towel rubbing her face clean of tears.

The open-mouthed ghouls looked back at her. Mouthed the taunt at her.

Gwei ar.

"Lei that's enough," her mother's voice cut through, "Steven is Harriet's partner lah."

"Gweilo don't know how to do a hard day's work. All they do is complain and give up!"

"You talking about Harriet's father?"

Auntie Pui-Ling pretended to spit on the floor, cursing loudly. "Don't you bring up that sei gweilo! He divorced you as soon as there was trouble."

"That's enough. He's still Harriet's father."

"Deem ar? Look at her? Her Cantonese is rubbish and she had kids without getting married! What side of the family do you think she picked that up from?"

She was nine years old again, a tug of war rope in a game with only one possible outcome. Harriet dropped her phone, the corner smacking off the tiled floor and cracking the screen. The table of relatives erupted in a fuss of advice and condolences, the argument forgotten.

She was coaxed back to the table, almost at the plastic stool, when she remembered the faces. Harriet turned, glaring towards the shrine in defiance of any mocking screams. The vase was gone.

"What's wrong ar?" Uncle Freddie asked.

"Did you see something, did you see *her*? The gwei?" said her auntie.

"No, I... it's nothing," Harriet replied, swallowing hard.

❋

Harriet had burned joss papers in the barbeque pit with her por-por when she was young. It had been fun, rolling up the gold sheets and tucking in the corners to look like the boat-like gold ingots. She would fan out the joss paper notes with their multiple zeroes, money for the afterlife, and throw it onto the fire. And would it just appear in the afterlife on someone's lap, in their spirit bank account or raining from the sky? The details were never very clear, even when Por-por tried to explain.

But the scale of things was different here. The street was full of religious goods shops, the smell of sandalwood pungent in the air from the bundles of joss sticks. Paper signs in red and gold for double happiness, studying, health and everything in between, decorated the walls between each small shop, advertising their wares on every available surface. It was chaotic on the surface, piles and heaps of goods spilling from shopfronts onto the pavement. But there was pride in it. Cardboard lined the ground and cellophane covered delicate items. One shopkeeper was cleaning with a dog-eared feather duster and another wiping each statue's face clean.

An elaborate papier-mâché house, a doll's house her Mia would've wanted, sat on a low table: candy floss pink over three floors with a balcony, twin turrets and external columns. Next to it, but not on the same scale, were card and paper TVs, smartphones, a hot tub, mahjong table, massage chair and tea-set. Child-sized cars lined streets outside the next shop: Porsches, BMWs and Audis with lucky license plate numbers of 18s and 88s. Cardboard handbags and shoes, perfumes and make up sets, gold and diamond watches and banquet meals: all boxy facsimiles but as good as the counterfeits in the market.

If she didn't know why they were here, she might have presumed they were Christmas shopping for kids.

"Is this all for burning?" Harriet asked her mother incredulously.

"Yes, I have a list of things your por-por definitely wanted, but you can choose the extras. A few nice outfits, some jewellery. Not the cheap stuff leh, I want to treat her," her mother said.

The row of red-faced Guan Yu statues watched Harriet as she drifted over, her mother's words rattling inside her head. Treat her? Not the cheap stuff? She looked down and sure enough, there was a price difference between the cardboard watch sets dependent on brand. Her voice broke in a sharp laugh. Great – days of insomnia, an upset stomach due to change in diet, not to mention washing herself with buckets of tepid water because her relatives had used up all the hot water – had rendered her into a hysterical madwoman.

The old woman dusting looked at her suspiciously, moving forward. "You Chinese?" she said in way of a greeting.

"My mother's from Hong Kong, my father's British," Harriet responded in Cantonese, the phrase so often repeated that it burned into her memory.

"Oh, half, you're a *half* wor!" she pronounced. Harriet grimaced and closed her eyes. No matter what side of the world she was on, people always thought this was the best way to describe her. Like a made-to-order pizza, split down the middle and dissected: the liver and left kidney for England, the stomach definitely Chinese, lactose-intolerance and all.

Harriet smiled through gritted teeth and moved on. Down the street, drawn towards the shop with ceramics. A whole two shelves were blue and white porcelain: vases with round bellies like a laughing Buddha, others tall necked like thin saplings, ones with a nipped-in waist, lidded jars and tiny teacups that could only be held with finger and thumb. They were patterned with dragon and phoenix pairs, willowy fairy ladies and plum blossom branches. Her eyes roved, looking for one with a pattern like the one she had broken.

There had been flower heads on it, small petals connected by curved stems that she remembered tracing with a finger. She would start at the top of the vase and see if she could make one unbroken trail to the bottom. If she could, if she could manage it, then everything would be okay. Mum and Dad would get back together, she wouldn't have to go to Chinese lessons anymore and her por-por could be a normal gran who made roast chicken rather than chicken feet for tea. As long as she could make a line – it would be true.

Three rows deep, she saw a vase with a familiar shape. The light did not quite penetrate between the shelves but she felt it in her bones, calling to her. Carefully she began to move the other porcelain to one side, the bases scraping on the metal shelving as she inched them away. Her fingers could just about touch the cool surface. See the shadow of a pattern.

The darker patches weren't quite the flower heads she had thought. Clouds? She turned the vase with one outstretched finger. Turned and saw it now. A face. A decapitated head lolling on the shelf.

"Shit!" Harriet said, jumping back.

"What are you doing?" the stall holder shouted, sandals slapping down the aisle. "You break, you pay!"

"No, no, I just saw..." Harriet shivered and looked back. Nothing but dust.

"Gwei? You see a ghost?" he asked, crouching beside her. Harriet shone her phone light left and right, but there was no third row of porcelain, just some cardboard boxes and empty space.

"No!" Harriet said, the negative burning her mouth. She saw the faces of her disappointed uncles and aunties lingering in the air. Then there was just the face of the exasperated stall holder, arms folded as he yelled at her to stop wasting his time. "Chi seen gweipor!"

They stopped for soup noodles and fishballs. The server waited for them impatiently, tapping her pencil on the table as Harriet's mum translated as much of the menu as she could from the peeling signs on the walls. The cook stared from behind his glass prison, steam wafting up as he pulled off the lid from a vat of soup and shook handfuls of noodles into wire baskets. Roasted ducks and strip of marinated meat were displayed like a hanging.

"Wonton noodles," Harriet decided finally.

"I translated all of that and you *still* pick wonton?" her mum said, frowning. "This place has stewed tripe!"

"No way," Harriet said. "Besides I like wonton noodles. They remind me of childhood. And Por-por..."

Her mum relented, ordering for them both as the

server repeated the order in a loud bark to the cook and threw two cups of lukewarm tea down on the table.

Por-por had made pork and prawn wonton. Taught her how to squeeze the little yellow squares into parcels and watch them bob on the surface of the hot water. And she remembered trailing water around the table with her finger unnoticed as everyone's attention was on her father, two bulging suitcases and a door, not slammed as expected, but politely and firmly closed behind him. His house keys still on the breakfast bar next to her elbow. How will he get back home? How will he get in when we are asleep? Harriet had asked and asked, following her mother around with the questions that rolled into her head and could not be ignored, like a small stone in her shoe, rattling and jagged no matter where she went. Por-por had made Harriet a distracting bowl of noodles and let her eat them with a fork. Come home, come home, what's left for you here, Por-por had said. I'll look after Harriet, she won't be a burden to you. We can teach her how to be Chinese. Soft but persistent, the message continued through the remaining months of her stay.

Harriet looked around the place, distracting herself from the tight lump forming in her throat. The old man in the corner had a simple plate of choi sum and was enjoying an unwieldy newspaper, folding and tucking it down to size so that he could bring it close to his face as he read. The aunties were washing the chopsticks in hot water, each shouting over each other about their sons' school grades. And there was also a young family sharing two portions of ho fun between four bowls.

It could be normal for her, easy if she knew just a little

bit more of the language, the culture, the people. Instead it was like she was on a rickety old light bus, hurtling through the Hong Kong streets and being dazed by the neon lights, but never stopping long enough for her to orientate herself.

"Have you seen her?" her mum asked.

"Her?"

"Por-por."

"Not this again," Harriet said, burying her hands in her hair.

"You didn't want to see the body. This is the best way to say goodbye!" her mother insisted.

"I'm not a child," Harriet replied. "You can't just make up stories about river dragons and a rabbit on the moon. You can't honestly tell me you've seen her ghost. A real gwei."

"Does it matter?"

"Of course, it matters."

"Uncle Lei is talking about something other than the money he lent Uncle Freddie two years ago. Auntie Pui-Ling has not criticized my weight once whilst she's been here. We remember your por-por, together, that's what's important."

Before Harriet could respond, their conversation was interrupted by the server dumping the two bowls of soup noodles. Harriet stuck her finger in the puddle of spilt water. She didn't know what to say. A reflection of the bowl blurred as she trailed a track through the liquid as she had done as a child. The angry child with no clear outlet for her grievances than a mother who wasn't like all the other mums at the school gate.

"It's different for me. It will always be different," Harriet said. Her chopsticks had twisted themselves up a little, crossing over in the way that Por-por would have scolded her for.

"Only if you let it be," her mother said.

The blue and white border on her soup bowl was inching very slowly around the rim. Hiding from her. Harriet turned it, hot broth scalding her hand although the pain barely registered. Ornate symmetrical patterns swirled before her, just out of focus as she turned and turned to follow the blasted thing, the mocking laugh just around the corner. Chasing it, head down near the table, following the trail.

"Harriet?"

The eyes looked frightened, Por-por's eyes, hiding from her around the next curve.

"Harriet!" her mother said, grabbing her arm. "What are you doing? Can you see her?"

Harriet released her hold on the bowl, suddenly aware the other people were looking at her, whispering that ubiquitous word under their breaths.

Gwei.

"No, I can't see anything."

"See lah," her mother said.

"That's your thumb obscuring the camera lens," Harriet said, glancing at the photo.

"No, that's your por-por's spirit wor. We need to help her cross over to the other side," she said. It was hard to argue when she, and all the other close relatives, were wearing the traditional funeral clothes Harriet had only seen in ancient TV dramas. A bandana across her forehead and a shapeless white tunic. They were in Por-por's village for the funeral, the old family home that Uncle Lei had inherited. It was like a different country out here in the rural dust, the houses large and sprawling compared to the box-room flat they had been staying in.

"Okay, okay. Tell me what I need to do," Harriet said.

"Here's the thing," her mother said, suddenly dropping her gaze and finding her jade bangle very interesting, "you aren't actually allowed to do the ceremony."

"What?" Harriet said. Her voice came out shriller than intended. They had been up all night making dish after dish in the sweltering kitchen for Por-por's afterlife feast. Lack of sleep had worn her patience to nothing. Her vision pushed in a little at the edges, pressing on her skull.

"The monk said so."

"Because I'm half?"

"No lah, because you aren't married," her mother said.

"How is that better?" Harriet heard herself snap. She took a deep breath.

Her mother sighed, shrugging her narrow shoulders. "Your por-por's spirit might be jealous, might want to come back. And... an unmarried woman is easier to possess."

"And if I was married, I'd *belong* to someone else, you mean?" Harriet said pointedly.

"Look, I don't make the rules! Best not to risk it lor. You can stay out here and burn the joss papers."

"It's just stupid. Stupid superstitious nonsense, and you know it!"

"This is part of *your* culture. Chinese tradition."

"Only fifty percent," she said. The words lingered in the humidity between them.

Only the cicadas broke the prevailing silence. Her mother made a strangled sound of frustration and turned to join the other aunties and uncles around the trefoil coffin. Uncle Lei whispered urgently to her, rolling his eyes a little. Harriet knew exactly what he would be saying. *Gwei. Gweipor, gwei sing.* Like chattering pigeons peck, peck, pecking at her. Harriet thought about leaving. She imagined the whole process in her mind's eye: getting a taxi, picking up her passport, buying an earlier ticket home. But her feet remained firmly planted, her limbs refusing to leave the shade of the trees.

The funeral started, the Buddhist monk leading in low stylized Cantonese that could have been Russian for all Harriet recognised. Her uncle's shoulders were shaking and for a moment Harriet was going to call out, scared he was having a fit. But then his wife started weeping loudly, like she was wringing the tears from a face cloth. Soon everyone was crying, howling wails and ugly hiccupping sobs filled with bubbles of snot smeared on cuff sleeves. Only her mother was silent. Her eyes were wet, but her fists tightly pressed to her sides and she kept her lips pressed firmly together. Harriet remembered now, where she had seen that expression before, the night Por-por had finally left the UK.

The monk told them to turn away, not to look lest the hungry spirit seek solace in a still warm body. Harriet looked instead at the trees behind the house. From low hanging branches dripped heavy roots, fingers digging down into the earth. The aerial roots swayed like curtains, the darkness between the forming shapes. It pulled at her, dragging her down with it as she heard them lower the coffin into the ground. She swayed forward, stumbling as she pinched herself on the inner arm to stay awake. The smell of incense, ripe fruit and the dishes they had cooked mingled in the growing heat, the heady concoction swirling in Harriet's sinuses. She dragged her glance away from the shifting tree, from the faces she could see watching her there, and stared instead at the backs of heads.

They started burning the bigger items in a huge bonfire. The joss papers caught fire, bright flashes of light before withering into grey soot. Ash rose, dancing coyly into the air above the large burner before tumbling like first snowfall into her hair and eyes. After the third cardboard flat screen TV, Harriet began to wonder which room Por-por would put it in, and if her afterlife mansion had enough plug sockets. The threads began to unravel the more she considered it: glasses, a toothbrush and traditional Chinese medicines. Did ghosts need a safe for valuables? Banks? For a woman who had lived plainly in life, Por-por's funeral offerings were decadent beyond reason. There were piles of paper notes to burn, skyscraper columns like the harbour skyline, and they had to be burned as individual sheets. After a while, Harriet's admiration of the handiwork, her morbid curiosity gave way to numb reflex and her hands fed things into the flames with the barest of recognitions.

With a sense of inevitability, Harriet looked for the blue and white among the piles of cardboard. The more they burned, the more she could feel its baleful gaze. Eyes had winked at her but disappeared when she turned to look. Among the clothing sets, a wide smile snapped shut when she grabbed it, holding only a joss paper handbag. But when she finally found it, the faces on the vase stared straight back at her. Deep blue eyes, one bigger than the other, held her gaze as they drooped on the surface of the cardboard. One, no two, three of them, drifting downwards with absurd crescent moon smiles as if to ooze onto her feet. She dropped it, flinching like the flames were already alight.

"Harriet?" her mum asked, suddenly at her side. "Did you see something?"

"Ghosts aren't real," Harriet whispered. The paper vase was just flowers and leaves. And there was a body burning on the pyre. A woman with preposterously pink skin in a simple cheongsam, her skin blistering in the heat and peeling off in layers. "Tell me you see that," she said softly.

"That's just a paper servant," her mother said.

Harriet started laughing. Unrestrained laughter punctuated by exhaustion, tears rolling down her cheeks as she continued. Laughing at the absurdity, the heat, the isolation she had felt as soon as her plane had landed.

Faces. All she could see were faces, uniform in their difference from her own.

"I'm glad she wasn't crying in the ceremony like that," Auntie Pui-Ling said, "You'd be fired as a professional mourner for that performance!" They had emerged now, her aunties and uncles in the white garb, surrounding her like clucking hens.

"I can see her," Harriet finally admitted to no-one in particular. She wasn't talking about the body burning in the fire. That was no more than paper and card like the rest. She meant the real ghost. The one who pulled the blanket over her shoulder after she had cried herself to sleep. That had sent her letters she could not read, and never had the energy to decipher. That hung her photo on the centre of the wall, in the biggest frame. That had kept every childhood gift she had sent on the shelf just below Guanyin's shrine.

Harriet picked up the paper vase, meeting the eyes of the faces.

"Yes," her mother said. And a press of bodies surrounded her, bony shoulders and soft limbs pushed in close. Comforting.

Harriet rubbed her eyes, stinging from the tears and the smoke. When she looked up, the courtyard had changed. The bonfire, the relatives, the noise – all gone. Her vision was unclear, like gazing through a crack in the door. Stacks of gold ingots were laid out like bamboo steamers on top of each other. Two lines of servants formed a path in front of her, each with a tray before them: tea and rambutan and tongyuan all on offer. Harriet moved forward towards the mansion at the end.

It had jade green dragon-spine ridges and flying eaves curving upwards. The cars they had burned were parked outside, with the showroom gleam on their bonnets.

The pink sky rained with fluttering bank notes like snow and Harriet reached out to catch them. The money was warm to the touch and smoky, some still singed with holes that mended themselves before her eyes. Inside the house, half a sofa was forming, and a small dog bounded across the polished tile floor. And there, in the kitchen, looking through the cupboards was a familiar figure, bent over and making pleased sounds under her voice.

"Por-por?" Harriet said. She reached out. A vase, blue and white porcelain, appeared in her hands.

"Por-por?" she repeated.

The old woman turned.

Harriet blinked, suddenly facing the bonfire, her eyes smarting. The joss paper vase watched her from the ground where she had dropped it. The chrysanthemum flowers had Por-por's eyes. Her mother stood beside her, the soothing weight of her presence giving Harriet a certain calmness.

She placed the vase within the flames.

WHAT CAN YOU DO ABOUT A MAN LIKE THAT?

Tim Major

✻

The dry leaves on the ground before a distant, sparse woodland produced a faint hush of movement. Molly prayed that nobody would be tempted to trample them.

Between Molly and the woodland there was a field of cattle. She could perceive the shuffle of the cows and even one of them rubbing its flank against a loose gate. No mooing, she noted. From behind her she heard – but tried not to hear, tried to suppress by willpower alone – the muted tink of cutlery on canteen trays, a murmur of conversation punctuated by barked commands and the occasional trill of laughter.

The loudest and most fascinating sound came from the heap of fabric that lay on the grass, frame left. The deflated hot air balloon was partially obscured, visually and aurally, by the eight-foot-square basket which pinned down the fabric. The breeze flicked at the nylon, raising it like a ghoul, occasionally discovering a way within the envelope to billow it out triumphantly, momentarily jostling the heavy basket. Molly closed her eyes, focused on the sound, captured it, committed it to memory. She heard thuds and a swelling like the sea in amongst the gasps of gusts, and behind it, beneath and above it, the shuffling sigh of wind within the valley and something harsher higher, and the occasional faraway call of gulls – did different types sound distinct? – and, smothering all of that, the sounds of thoughtless humans.

She spun around, glared at the crew bus and the canteen van. Thoughtless. A pair of male extras toppled out of the bus, trays in their hands, bumping torsos in a mock-fight to be first to leave. She only needed a few minutes without all of *that*. Was it so much to ask?

She heard Andrus Jay's footsteps on the grass. Nobody but the director trod with such assurance.

"You look lost," Andrus said.

"I'm listening."

"To?"

Molly gestured at the trapped hot air balloon, the fields, the valley, the sky. Andrus still watched her expectantly.

She shook her head. "Nothing."

She watched the scene play out for the fourth time from far behind and to one side of the monitor screens, headphone cushions pressed tight onto her ears, fingers resting on the faders of the mixing console upon her knees, staring at the actors rather than their onscreen facsimiles, absorbing the tone of the real world.

It was a crucial scene, Andrus had insisted, a turning point in Ralph's character arc. Ralph would now begin to understand that his ability to control a situation was not predetermined and not dependent on his wealth. To commandeer a hot air balloon was a grand gesture, but foolhardy.

But following a truncated third take and a hiatus during which Andrus paced and pointed, something had changed. As the characters Ralph and Jessie tumbled from the basket, Jessie's foot caught, she squealed, and the pair fell bundled in the nylon fabric, she on top of him, apologising even as their stomachs touched. Molly winced at the rasping rustles from the radio mics hidden in the folds of the actors' clothes, which had never been intended to make contact. She heard a hum, a hiss of ropes, a distant reverberating cough that made her grimace. When the interference ended, she pushed up the feed from the boom mic. The bodies on the nylon produced an array of fidgeting sounds; a pleasing puzzle that she relished solving in post-production.

The scene ended and Andrus shouted something and applauded. The hopeless fan Jessie Anderson became the former Channel 4 morning TV presenter Camilla Kendall-Roper. The famous singer Ralph Dines became the famous actor Theo Marshall.

It was a wrap and Molly had to leave *now*.

※

If the sitting room had had a fourth wall, its acoustics – its room tone – would undoubtedly have been warm. In post-production, rather than reproduce the environmental sound as it really was, Molly's task would be to generate a sound to match the location as it appeared in the onscreen fiction. Yet to construct a notional fourth wall would mean starting afresh, as any dialogue recorded live would be inextricably bound to the acoustics she heard now. So why record any of the actors' speech at all, here on set?

In fact, there were no actors present at this moment. Even the tungsten lamps were turned off, making them spindly, dark trees on their stands; only the overhead fluorescents provided dim, diffuse light. A handful of staff would still be in the building somewhere, poring over tomorrow's schedules or taking flak from Agnès the producer. But here in the studio it was what anybody but Molly would call silent.

She pulled back her left headphone cup to rest behind her ear, in order to listen to both the recorded output and the real world. Then she flicked through presets and archive files on her digital recorder, attempting to find a rough match for the acoustics of the room. After several minutes of tinkering she found one close enough that once there were bodies on set in the morning it might be almost perfect. She glanced down to check the LCD screen, then exhaled when she saw that the sound from her headphones wasn't a factory preset but one of her own recordings. It was the ambient sound within her parents' house – their sitting room, in fact, the room in which she had spent her childhood, in which her dad's ancient reel-to-reel recorder had exerted a pull, a fascination, and in which she had crouched on the carpet making a nest of trimmed tape, splicing together music and her family's conversations, building something new and strange and more wonderful than the world around her.

She had made the recording only last year, but her parents had never rearranged the furniture, had never even moved the framed pictures on the walls. The room tone was precisely as it had always been. This was the sound of the past.

She heard an alien hum, a sharp hiss, a distant cough. She pulled down the headphones.

Camilla Kendall-Roper appeared at left of frame, tying up her hair.

"Oh. I didn't think anybody was here," she said. Her cheeks were flushed.

"I didn't think anybody was here either."

Molly smiled – she had meant nothing by it – but Camilla blinked rapidly. "You're the microphone girl, aren't you?"

Molly shrugged. She was thirty-three. "Sound designer. Same thing."

Camilla craned her neck to peer into the darkness, perhaps checking if anybody else might be lurking there. Her eyes shone. She fiddled with the top button of her shirt, which was already buttoned. "How do you design sound? It's not like you can see it, touch it."

"It's just one of those things. If it's not done right, you'd know if when you watched the film. Something would be off. I could explain it if you like."

Another glance into the black. "Actually, there's probably a taxi waiting."

"No worries. It was nice to meet you."

Camilla flashed a white smile but made no eye contact. "Yeah. Look, I'd rather you didn't—" Then her hair said *shush* as she shook her head, and her heels tapped her away, eleven clacking steps, carrying her through a soundproof door that gulped with the suction of its rubber seal.

Molly heard another sound, in the direction from which Camilla had appeared. Fabric, metal, the buzz of a strap being threaded and tightened.

The stage set beyond Jessie's family's sitting room was a hotel bedroom, implicitly a five-star affair. It had no door but from around the plywood wall appeared Theo Marshall. He tucked his belt into the trouser loop with a snick.

Molly backed away, out of the pool of fluorescent light.

"Who's that?" Theo said, his voice carrying across the space, surfing the reverb, immune from echo.

Molly didn't move.

"You. Peeping Tom."

He strode across the sitting room, bumping into and shifting one armchair and then the other, creating continuity issues for tomorrow. "Come on out. I have you in my sights."

A hum, a hiss, a cough.

Molly stepped forward on shaky legs.

Theo's white shirt was crumpled and there were sweat stains at the armpits. He scratched at the stubble on his chin (tomorrow morning Makeup would shave it to precisely the same length it had been at the start of today's filming) and Molly could hear the ugly gravel sound of it though he was still several paces away.

He stopped where the light was brightest, an actor's instinct. "Have you been snooping upon me?"

Molly pointed to her headphones around her neck. "Working."

"It's very late. You're diligent. A busy bee."

"I find it easier when I'm alone."

Theo smirked, perhaps having detected a double-entendre than Molly couldn't identify.

"And what nature of work is that?"

Molly shivered and at first she didn't know what, precisely, had spooked her. Then she understood. Abruptly, all she could hear was Theo's carefully-enunciated stage voice, as if somebody had closed the faders on all the other sounds, the ambience reduced to absolute silence. She exhaled with relief when the room tone re-established itself, though her heartbeat in her ears was louder. Still, that was *her* sound and she would take what she could get.

"I record sound," she said. "I record voices – your voice – but everything else too. It's just as a reference, really. Andrus's camera setup means I can't get in close with a boom mic, so it's radio mics for dialogue, and that'll only be of use as a blueprint. The real work will be in ADR, months down the line. But anything I can capture at this stage will be useful. Even the sounds of empty rooms."

Theo brought out his phone, thumbed at it. "Interesting. Which is your favourite?"

"My favourite sound?"

A half-smile: it might have meant *Who cares?* or something else. "Your favourite empty room."

"I've only just got started. So far, I've been wrapped up in the location footage. Studio work is more contained but less my thing."

"Funny. I'm an indoor person at heart. Have we met before?"

"I pin on your radio mic every day."

"Before that."

"I don't remember."

Theo put his hands on his hips, clucked his tongue. He was taller than her by almost a foot. He always had been.

A hum, a hiss, a cough.

"May I?" he said. He reached out, plucked her headphones from her head, his shirt cuffs tapping lightly against the plastic. Molly caught a whiff of something sickly sweet but that was nothing compared to the invasive loudness of the cable dragging against her short hair and scraping along the arm of her glasses.

She felt absurdly grateful when Theo took the digital recorder, too, so that she was no longer tethered to him.

Theo listened and frowned. "There's nothing there." He peered at the readout. "Chicken Cottage, ten fifty-two p.m., Friday twelfth Dec, oh-nine. Ah, of course! I hear it now. A fat fryer, I suppose? And maybe a till opening. No dialogue though, a worrying sign close to pub chuck-out on a Friday." He turned the device over in his hands. "I presume this gadget records too?"

Molly nodded.

Theo clicked the red button; Molly felt very aware that although it was impossible for him to overwrite anything by doing so, he couldn't have known that. He held up the recorder and spoke into the twin microphones that emerged sideways from its top like a facsimile of his smile.

"This is Theo Marshall speaking," he said, enunciating deliberately, speaking loudly due to the headphones still covering his ears. "And this message – my voice itself – is a gift to the very appealing young sound girl—" He raised a perfect eyebrow.

"Molly Liáng."

"Molly Leanne."

Theo pushed the stop button but didn't return the device.

"We're actually the same age," Molly said.

That smirk. "Is that so? You obviously pay close attention. To me. I tell you what, shall we explore some other empty rooms?"

"No. Please give me back my equipment."

Theo handed it back to her distractedly, then walked straight past Molly and into the gloom, but not in the direction of the exit.

She hesitated, weighing up her options. She found that she didn't fear him, exactly.

She stepped into the darkness. He had disappeared.

"In here!" Theo's head emerged from a tall crate with metal braces, raised on pneumatic legs. "Have you seen this thing yet?"

Molly ignored the hum, the hiss, the cough, and climbed into the crate. No inner voice explained to her what she thought she was doing.

Theo was sitting in the driver's seat. The only light was the glow of the dashboard. The window was opaque and painted green; exteriors would be added later as VFX. Behind the seats was a mess of pneumatic cables and scuffed chrome boxes with switches and dials. During filming, she presumed some unlucky crew member would be crouched there, timing the jolts and simulating swerves and turns to match Theo's steering.

"It's my own car, you know," Theo said, tapping the Bentley winged logo in the centre of the steering wheel. At his feet was a box with a single metal button; he stomped on it in sync with his mimed turning of an imaginary key in the ignition, producing an engine purr and a simulated rumble of the seats. "The real one is. Did you know I've loaned it to the production? It's the least I can do to support a small-budget setup like this. And having this replica constructed is a delight. I've never actually driven my car myself, so sitting here in this seat is something of an adventure. I do believe I know you, Molly."

Molly bent to her digital recorder. "Please be quiet, just for a minute."

In the film the situation would be the same, in aural terms: Theo and a woman, Camilla, who was taller but of a similar build to Molly. Molly initiated the recording but listened to the location raw rather than via the headphones. The faint growl of the fake engine not entirely masking the close, low, buzz of pneumatic equipment on standby. The audible discomfort of Theo so close to her left shoulder, his shuffling to settle himself in the seat. She listened, captured, committed to memory.

A hum, a hiss.

Theo stifled a cough and held up a hand in apology.

Molly nodded.

"Have you seen what else it can do?" Theo said.

Molly kept the recording running, noting the reverberation of Theo's voice around the cabin. She didn't want to speak, but of course Camilla would speak, so she made herself say, "What else can it do?" checking the LED level markers on the recorder as she did so.

Theo flashed perfect teeth and leaned back with his arm draped into the gap between them. Molly heard a click.

The cabin spasmed on its pneumatic legs. Molly gripped her recorder in one hand, the dashboard with the other.

Another film-star grin, another sharp *tock*.

The dashboard shuddered.

Molly yelped as the fascia of the dashboard bent and then cracked along previously invisible lines, pushing against the palm of her hand and then her knees as it crumpled. Beside her Theo sucked in his stomach to allow the steering wheel to spring towards him. The rim of the windscreen shrieked and twisted and the roof of the car groaned with torsion. The shards of glass would be added in post-production.

✳

"*Theo Marshall?* You lucky fucker," Leanne said, then glanced at the toddler in the pram, whose eyelids continued to slide closed against the stripes of autumn sunlight.

"He's not so great," Molly said quietly.

"Maybe not. But he was, back in his *Mean Time* days. And perhaps he will be again, after rehab, et cetera. How's he looking?"

"Okay. Overconfident."

Leanne stopped, chewing her lip. Her son, Christopher, made a consonant sound, and she hurriedly resumed pushing the pram. "I think that's what I always found appealing about him. That absolute confidence. I bet he's tall."

"He is tall, yes."

Leanne pushed and thought; Molly walked beside her and heard. A leaf had caught in one wheel of the pram, introducing a scuff to its regular rumble. The intermittent low light shining through the avenue of trees on the riverside almost made her shut her eyes, like Christopher in his pram. She wondered if she could navigate via echolocation, if she had to, judging the distance of the sounds of the river and the hooting of students on its far bank from the echoes from the railings to her right.

Amid a patch of shade she saw that Leanne was watching her closely. Leanne had always been able to read her, back in their university days, when they were so close that people had refused to call Molly by her surname, Liáng, instead replacing it with Leanne. Theo's replication of the name had been a coincidence; he couldn't have known about that.

"I often think of you, when I'm out and about," Leanne said. "When I hear something I know you'd want to record and add to your collection. Are you going to invite me to the première?"

"If you like. It'll be next summer at the earliest. Lots of work to do yet. During filming, I'm basically listening. Most of the sounds – most of the dialogue, even – that you'll hear in the finished film haven't been created yet."

"I was remembering that mindfulness class that you came along to, before he was born." Leanne nodded towards the sleeping Christopher. "When we were told to concentrate on every single sound we could hear. It was like my ears were getting – I don't know, *bigger* – hearing stuff from miles away. Dogs barking, the ring-road, all that, even though we were still right there in that pokey treatment room."

Molly nodded. "Your ears are better than any microphone. If you'd wanted to record all that sound, to keep it forever, you couldn't have. Instead you'd have to recreate it as closely as possible."

Leanne frowned and they plodded along the path without speaking. Molly heard the swish of their jackets – Leanne's tweed and her scudding raincoat – and the clack of Leanne's heels and her own padding footsteps in soft-soled boots; the chatter of pedestrians and a child's faint wail, the rattle of bikes on the bridge ahead and the grind of a drill far away; the distant chaos of a recycling lorry being filled with glass, the lap of water and the lopsided void of the uninterrupted air above the river. And – yes – the barking of a small dog and the constant drone of the ring-road, and she wondered whether or not her friend was listening too.

"So, what's this film about anyway?"

Molly sighed. "It's called *The Weekend to End All Weekends*. And it's probably shit."

"Why are you doing it then?"

"Money. And I'm only sound. If the dialogue's audible, and I don't disrespect the score, and I hold back from adding comedy swanee whistles to the soundtrack, everyone'll be happy and I'll get paid." Leanne was watching her again. Molly puffed her cheeks. "You see right through me, don't you? The film was better when I read the script. It's about this famous singer, and he's just finished a triumphant homecoming concert, or something. And there's this bit where he gets trapped in a dressing room – not his own – and then the power goes out and his people think he's already left, and the person who eventually lets him out is this adoring fan of his called Jessie."

"Played by Camilla Kendall-thingy."

"Yep. And this singer, Ralph, he's a decent guy, or at least so our director insists. It's late and he's grateful, so after a bit of bluster he offers Jessie a lift home in his swanky car, which means driving from Manchester to Cumbria somewhere. But on the motorway there's a pileup and the car's crushed."

She shuddered, remembering the groaning, crumpling replica of Theo's car, the claustrophobia upon claustrophobia, despite the fact that she had left the studio immediately and Theo hadn't hounded her. He probably thought of himself as a decent guy, too.

"Do they die? Is it a ghost story?"

"Ralph's fine. Jessie is injured. Cut to a private room in hospital and there's Ralph at the bedside; he's been there all night. And then there's some bit of business which was muddled in the script and can only get more muddled when we film it, but the upshot is that Ralph is informed that there's a shard of glass embedded in Jessie's heart. It's inoperable without killing her, but she's going to die anyway, in a day or two."

"That doesn't sound too plausible."

"Andrus, the director, muttered something about magical realism when I said that. I don't think he knows what magical realism is."

"Bit weird," Leanne said. "And how does Jessie react?"

Molly reached out her foot to dislodge the leaf from the axle of the pram, restoring the happy trundle of the wheels upon the tarmac warped by roots that made tiny wooden speed bumps and produced corresponding huffs of noise.

"That's the thing," she said. "Jessie's oblivious about her heart. Ralph discharges her from hospital – who the hell knows how – and then he makes this decision that's pivotal to the plot but, frankly, is insane. He decides to show Jessie the best weekend imaginable. That is, the best weekend *he* can imagine that she might imagine. Which means spending it all with him. Meals in Michelin-starred restaurants, dancing, him feigning falling for her, this hot air balloon ride where he pays off the operator to pilot it himself. But then in the second act it goes wrong, of course. Molly challenges him – she's not so adoring a fan that she can't see that the whole situation is pretty unlikely – and then she runs off, and Ralph gets into a fight around the back of some pub, but then finally proves himself to Jessie by making a fool of himself serenading her drunkenly in public, which ruins his reputation. At least that's how it was in the script. It was called *Ride to the Abyss* back then."

"Why the change?"

"Theo Marshall came on board. And it's canny casting – after all his escapades he's a dead ringer for this deluded, vain, soon-to-be-washed-up singer. But of course the producer didn't see it that way, and the director can talk himself into any amount of nonsense. So Ralph is no longer deluded. He's kind and he's doing his best, and he falls for Jessie for real, and when he serenades Jessie in Ulverston market square it's a pitch-perfect performance, or at least it will be with judicious auto-tuning."

"But there's a tragic end."

Molly snorted. "Not in this new draft. Turns out Ralph was given false information. I bet you anything Andrus will insert something heavy-handed about the doctor maybe actually being Cupid in scrubs. So Jessie's A-OK and Ralph's in love and cut to credits."

"Sounds like something I'd probably enjoy. You know, if you hadn't just ruined it for me."

Molly shook her head. "You don't see any issue with the premise?"

"It's just a bit of fluff."

"Put yourself in Jessie's position for a moment, would you? You're hours from death. Some guy you've never met decides not to tell you that fact. And he whisks you off on activities of his choosing, with the clock ticking. You don't think that's wrong?"

"But you said she's his biggest fan. What could be better?"

"Surely you'd prefer to make your own choices? If you were on the brink of death, mightn't you like to see your friends one last time, and your family? The presumption is just—" Molly's teeth chattered, the sound reverberating along her jaw and in her skull.

After several seconds Leanne said, "Still. You get to hang out with Theo Marshall."

The clacking of Molly's teeth was replaced by a hum that corresponded to nothing in the world around her. The pram wheels hissed as they raised spray from a puddle. She coughed and then she stopped on the path and she wasn't crying exactly, but sobbing and gasping silently.

Leanne hurriedly put the brake on the pram and then embraced her.

Only seconds later, Molly pushed her away gently. Christopher spluttered but then smacked his lips and slept again.

"I knew him," Molly said. "Back at sixth form. I mean, I didn't really know him at all. I was quiet; he was film-star material even then. Popular."

Leanne frowned. "Did you have some kind of a thing together? You told me that you didn't have any experience until uni."

Molly shook her head. "The only time I was ever near him was during a theatre production in the first year. He was the lead actor, of course, playing Stanley Kowalski with an unplaceable American accent – I don't think he's ever mastered it, not even on *Mean Time* for all those years on TV. And I was on sound. I desperately wanted to man the mixing desk, but instead I was backstage, clipping on the mics, even ending up helping with wardrobe changes, a dogsbody. And it only happened this one time – the opening night, if you want to call it that, although there were only three performances in total. Kowalski exited stage right and there I was in the wings, and Theo was all full of testosterone and applause. And I tried to help him with the mic and then... I remember the hum of people backstage, taking their jobs so seriously. The hiss of ropes as the stagehands got ready with the curtains and the backdrops needing switching for the scene change. Then a cough of somebody out in the auditorium, interrupting Blanche DuBois unpacking her suitcase. And Theo pressed me up against the wall, not my body or shoulders but my head with both his hands. And he kissed me too, an awful misdirected thing, maybe because he was so much taller and my face wasn't turned up to his. I remember the back of my head hurt and that somehow I couldn't move my hands to push him off and then *his* hand was somewhere else – down there – pressing hard through the front seam of my jeans. And all I could think was that I should shout, but the audience was only just settling into the play and I swear everything had gone completely silent and there's a sort of magic in that, in the theatre, isn't there?"

"Fuck," Leanne said. "Theo Marshall."

"Don't tell me I should consider myself lucky."

"No." Leanne gripped Molly's hands tight. "No. That's not lucky. Mol. Tell me you reported him."

"I never told anyone. And I kept out of his way and he never looked at me again."

"And now? I'm guessing you haven't challenged him."

"He doesn't even know who I am. I'm keeping out of his way, again."

Leanne put her hands on the pram, her gloves squeaking on its foam handles though she didn't resume pushing it.

"What did it do to you?"

Molly listened to her breathing, which was gradually returning to normal, a clean warm sigh through the nostrils. She shrugged.

After the end of filming Molly spent six weeks working on an animated TV show for children. The movement of the characters' mouths was intentionally abstract, which allowed for creating the dialogue track after the visuals had been signed off. She worked with a young boy and girl for more than a fortnight, more like play than work, riffing with them and even improvising lines to evoke performances full of enthusiasm and liveliness. When the children left the studio felt empty, haunted by their laughter, but Molly threw herself into incorporating sound effects into the mix, and developing environmental sounds that would evoke the alien worlds that the characters visited. It was a happy time, just Molly and her mixing desk, though every so often she would turn and gaze through the soundproof window into the empty studio, wondering if the hum, the hiss, the cough were real or just within her head.

On the morning of the sixteenth of November Molly turned on the TV to be told by the morning news presenters that Theo Marshall was dead. Later that morning Andrus Jay called her mobile phone.

"You heard, I'm guessing? Of course you heard."

"What does it mean?" Molly replied.

"It means he doesn't wake up tomorrow. It means he's another shining star snuffed out before his time. It means he won't be doing any interviews or red carpet appearances. But between you and me it also means there's renewed interest in our little movie. If it had been a car crash rather than a tawdry overdose – or even if there were any hint of suicide rather than him just keeling over at a celebrity bash – it might have been even bigger for us. Anyway, the upshot is that we have a new backer."

"Who?"

"No less than Netflix. I know, right?"

Molly let silence emphasise her lack of delight. "And you're going to tell me that they want it fast."

"We have a moment here, Molly. We have to capture it. We take too long, and the public will have moved on."

"Post-production starts in less than two weeks. Your decision to go multi-camera, because Theo Marshall couldn't be trusted to hit his marks, means that I have the worst – and I mean the *worst* – reference track imaginable. Three-quarters of the dialogue needs to be rerecorded. And our lead is dead."

"There's always a way."

Molly sighed. "Cut to the chase, Andrus. You've told me that time is tight. Will there be a bigger budget?"

A static-filled pause.

"No."

❊

"Are there any questions for our honoured guest?" Professor Richard Kemper said to the crowd.

There were only a dozen or so students in the small screening room. At first, none of them raised their hands. Molly reached for her satchel which she had leant against the side of the chair not visible to the audience. Her boots were scuffed and she felt very aware that most of the students were dressed in smarter clothes than she was.

"At the back," Richard said.

A female student wearing a mustard-coloured sweater raised herself from her seat to address Molly. "You've already told us about your career progression, but is there anything you can identify that distinguishes you from the crowd? Do you have any tips to stand out?"

Molly smiled. "I'm good. My CV is standard enough. I'm crap at approaching people at networking events. I didn't get a big break. I'm just good at what I do. It's not a great answer to your question, but it's true."

She was aware of Richard's sideways glance. Throughout the interview he had done a good job of reshaping her succinct, sometimes blunt, answers into soundbites palatable to his students, adding in his own lengthy anecdotes as padding and light relief.

"Over here," Richard said, pointing. "Yes, you."

"Which plug-ins do you consider indispensable?"

This time Molly answered at greater length, safe in the dry details of audio software. Pens scratched on notepads and faces were lit from beneath by phones.

"We have time for one more," Richard said.

"What's the point?" a male voice said. "What are you aiming to achieve?"

Molly searched out the man who spoke. He had a shaved head and a black T-shirt with the white logo of a record label.

"In career terms?" she asked.

"No."

Richard leaned forward. "I think we may as well interpret this question as relating to the fundamentals. We've heard about your childhood inspirations, Molly, your fascination with technology. But of course once you master the technology, once you're in a flow state in the studio, particularly when working alone, you're left with something else. Something that, presumably, continues to fascinate you. Is that fair to say?"

Molly nodded. "The puzzle."

"Which aspect?"

"The match. The systematic breaking down of a real soundscape and the building up of one that replicates it."

"And you don't consider that pedestrian? That is, the replacement of something real with something ersatz that, even if it reaches its apex, can only equal the original rather than surpass it?" When Molly didn't answer, he continued, "This goes all the way back to the use of sound in film in the infancy of the industry. The sheer scepticism of it. There's a quote I noted down but didn't find a way to shoehorn in earlier." He chuckled, then glanced down at the exercise book in his lap, but Molly suspected he had already committed the text to memory. "In 1929 René Clair wrote of 'talkie' audiences, 'They might have been leaving a music hall, for they showed no sign of the delightful numbness which used to overcome us after a passage through the silent land of pure images. They talked and laughed, and hummed the tunes they had just heard. *They had not lost their sense of reality.*' But then – forgive me – another quote I far prefer. Robert Bresson, this time. 'The ear goes more toward the within, the eye toward the outer'. So I put it to you, Molly, that this striving for replication is surface detail and quite possibly a Sisyphean task. Instead, incorporating hints of the aural environmental of a location – what Walter Murch called 'precipitant sounds' that represent rather than replicate an event – may actually be more powerful and more evocative than your attempts at fidelity."

Molly was occupied with the sound of her blood in her ears. "Is this still the preamble to a question, Professor Kemper?"

"Perhaps not. But it's important nonetheless. In emphasising the puzzle, as you call it, you may be missing something broader and more illuminating. You may be missing the opportunity to reveal the *inner*. If you had to pick between aural fidelity and inner truth, which would you choose?"

Molly thought of Theo Marshall and a hum, a hiss, a cough. To have captured every sound, every aspect of him, would have been to relegate him to a recording, something tangible that could be switched off as easily as on.

"Fidelity," she said. "Memory *is* truth."

After the interview ended Richard congratulated Molly and suggested drinks whilst helping her on with her jacket. Molly didn't refuse outright but asked after his wife and daughter and realised that she had already decided she would never encounter him again.

"Slower," Molly said. "Slow at the start, and build in volume."

"You may have helped me, and you may be stranded, but I can't make your safe delivery home my concern."

"Again, please. Hesitant, then growing in confidence."

Through the thick window she watched Colin Charles frown at the script. "You may have helped me," he said, with a new quaver in his voice, "and you may be stranded, but I can't make your safe delivery home my concern." He almost shouted the final part.

Molly resisted the impulse to let her head drop onto the mixing desk. "I'm going to play you the production track again, okay?"

She clicked the onscreen bookmark. The audio was hissy and uneven, and lacked the reverberation of sound passing through a space. When Theo spoke the line of dialogue, some part of his costume must have rubbed on the radio mic, creating intermittent thuds. But the tone of his delivery was still clear. Buried in his statement were traces of self-regard and swagger, neither of which had been the director's intention, but which were fundamental to the performance.

"You may have helped me, and you may be stranded, but I can't make your safe delivery home my concern," Colin said, staring up at the speakers, mimicking the intonation.

"You don't sound powerful."

"You may have helped me, and you may be stranded—"

"Stop. Sorry. Listen, I'm going to play you another version."

"Another take?"

"No. This is the take we need. I'm going to play you the environmental audio track, recorded through the boom. Concentrate on the *feel* of the line."

She brought up the track, clicked play. Theo's dialogue was barely discernible beneath the hum of ambient sound of the corridor outside the dressing room in which Ralph had found himself trapped. In "You may have helped me," she perceived guilt, then tentative hints of scorn in, "And you may be stranded." Then a pause of almost a second. Then, "But I can't make your safe delivery home my concern," with its full-throttle disdain, the ever-so-slight emphasis on 'safe' as opposed to the more obvious 'my'. Perhaps even Theo himself wouldn't have been able to replicate it.

"I think I've got it now," Colin said.

"I'll play it one more time, then you'll see the recording light."

Colin nodded along with the rhythm of the dialogue. In the pause after "You may be stranded," Molly heard a cough behind her, in the room rather than through the monitors. She turned and there was nobody there.

"You may have helped me, and you may be stranded," Colin said, his voice rising in pitch all the time. Then, too quickly, "But I can't make your safe delivery home my concern."

Molly scrunched up the schedule printout in her fist.

"Again, please," she said.

"It will be here somewhere," Rabiah said, prodding in a glass bowl with a long white fingernail.

Molly watched her bare shoulders, her long neck as she bent forward, her close-cropped black hair. If not for the tap of the fingernail on glass, the woman might have been a wraith. Molly had no idea if Rabiah was older than her – and older than Theo, by definition – or younger. She assumed, and then felt ashamed for assuming, that Rabiah was a catwalk model.

"I don't want to put you to any trouble," Molly said.

Rabiah turned. Her smile was genuine. Molly decided that she liked her, and that the awkward moments drinking tea in the sitting room of the mansion – which Theo had bought with his first wife – had been a product of forced convention.

"It is a more interesting request than the others I have heard these weeks," Rabiah said. "Look, here are the keys."

Rabiah led the way, her bare feet soundless on the marble tiles of the hallway. As they crossed the courtyard she and her trailing white dress were a silent void in the hum of the world. Rabiah looked around her when she entered the garage buildings. Molly wondered if she had ever been in this part of her home before.

Twin pips, and the indicator lights of the Bentley flashed in the dark.

"Would it be okay if we took it outside?" Molly said, her hand already placed over a button on the wall marked *Doors*. "Not out for a drive. Literally just outside."

Rabiah frowned, shrugged. "I don't drive." She held out the keys.

Molly eased herself into the driver's seat as the garage door swung open to create an accelerated dawn. She waited for Rabiah to enter, then started the engine. It barely made a sound she could describe, though the tone of the space became infused with something. Potential, or expectation, perhaps. She edged the car out of the garage, then brought it to a halt on the driveway. She closed her eyes, recalibrating the engine noise now that it was even quieter in the mix, no longer echoing from the walls of the garage.

"Were you his lover?" Rabiah said.

Molly stared at her. It was an honest question. A woman as magnificent as Rabiah had no business looking so uncertain.

"No."

"Something else?"

"I don't know what you mean."

"Lover is maybe the wrong word. Theo had women, I know that. He had them."

The emphasis on 'had' made the word reverberate within the car.

"I hardly knew him, I swear. I'm just trying to do my job."

A nod. "And your job is to make somebody sound like Theo."

"I want to make *Theo* sound like Theo. We have the visual. I need the sound."

Rabiah thought about this. "He considered his face his great... is the word 'asset'? Yes. Not his voice. Why do you care so deeply, Miss Liáng?"

"It's my job. I care about my job. And—"

Rabiah waited patiently.

There was an end to the sentence Molly had begun, but she couldn't speak it. *And without the sound to match his image, he will remain a ghost.*

"Is it okay if I have moment in here alone?" she said.

After barely any hesitation, Rabiah exited the car without a sound. She stood on the driveway at the periphery of Molly's vision, unmoving.

Molly watched the sky above the trees turn from orange to pink to blue. She heard the steady warm hum of the motor, the shifting of her shirt and skin against the seat fabric, her breath, her swallowing, her tongue wetting cracked lips.

Theo wasn't in the mix.

She rifled within her satchel, trying to ignore Rabiah's presence outside the car.

The track was already lined up and the Bluetooth speaker was already paired to the digital recorder. Theo's voice came from the speaker. "This is Theo Marshall speaking," he said, enunciating deliberately, and Molly remembered him raising his voice due to wearing her headphones. "And this message – my voice itself – is a gift to the very appealing young sound girl—" She saw him raise his eyebrow. She noted the consistency of his recorded voice, played back in this confined space. The claustrophobia, the amplification of potential, expectation, threat.

Then her own voice came from the speaker: "Molly Liáng."

His: "Molly Leanne."

In the moment before he clicked the stop button, she heard a hum, a hiss, a cough. He was here. She had summoned him. He was in the device in her hands and he was in the fabric of the car and he was in the driver's seat, *this* seat, and so where was she?

"I don't care," she said into her phone. She was standing at the end of the country lane that led to Theo's mansion, waiting for the taxi. She pushed at a pile of white-painted stones with her foot, enjoying the sound of her boot sole against the covering of lichen.

At the other end of the line a crackling Andrus said, "Agnès won't accept any further increase in ADR budget. You still have the rest of the cast to record and we're overspent already."

"It isn't my fault our lead actor accidentally went and killed himself."

"Colin Charles already headed back to London. He has a recurring role in some shitty ITV police procedural. Explain to me why you need to record Theo's lines again."

"We didn't capture him." Molly winced. "I mean, we didn't capture Theo's delivery accurately. Audiences will spot that it isn't his voice."

"They won't. They won't care, Molly."

"Get Colin back in. It doesn't matter how you pay for it. Take it out of my wages."

First up in the Monday schedule was Camilla Kendall-Roper. Her replication of the live-recorded lines was precise and yet full of the same warmth as her original delivery. She would go far as an actor. Success in the industry, for anyone other than bankable, untouchable stars, was as much related to reliability as raw talent or charisma.

Despite her calm performance, in which lines were often nailed on her first or second read, Camilla crumpled the moment Molly announced that she had everything she needed.

"Are you okay?" Molly said through the intercom.

Camilla turned away. The only sound was a faint sniffing.

Molly left the control room and pushed through the soundproof door. As she approached Camilla, the actor rose from her seat and met her halfway, somehow burying her slender body into Molly's embrace despite being so much taller.

"It's all right," Molly whispered. When Camilla didn't respond, she said it again, her voice made crisp by the baffles that reduced noise pollution within the studio, then again and again until the words became a drone with only the 's' and 't' sounds audible in a smooth tide of vowels.

"It isn't," Camilla said finally.

"Take a seat?"

"I probably should."

They sat facing each other on their swivel chairs.

"It's just hard," Camilla said. She rubbed the sleeve of her sweater against her face; Molly saw a glint of mucus on the pale wool. "Saying those lines again, imagining saying them to him."

"Theo."

A sorrowful nod.

Molly remembered her only previous encounter with Camilla, on the stage set that night. "You were close to him."

Camilla emitted a snort. Guiltily, Molly wished she had left the recording to run on; an ugly sound like that, a true reflection of hopelessness, would be impossible for an actor to simulate. A waste of a sound.

"Not close," Camilla said. "Unless you mean we fucked. We did fuck."

"You don't have to—"

"I didn't want to do it. He had a way about him. I didn't want to but he made it happen." She arched her back, blinking as if surprised at finding herself there, confiding in Molly. "And then after that, pretty much the only words we exchanged were via Ralph and Jessie. And then after that..." Her head hung. She gulped a breath, raised her face to Molly's, pride there now along with disgust. "I found out I was pregnant."

"Oh shit. Camilla." Molly held out her hands but Camilla didn't accept them. "Have you just found out?"

Camilla shook her head. "That was a lie, about not speaking to him again. Because I told him. He knew."

"Did the pregnancy have something to do with his death? Sorry, that's the wrong question."

"No chance," Camilla replied, her lopsided smile an acceptance of the apology. "He made it clear he didn't give that much of a toss. And anyway, he thought I'd aborted it. In fact, he ordered me to."

"I'm so sorry," Molly said.

"Don't be. It's crap, sure. And I'll be glad to be done with this film – I'll be damned if I'm going to promote it, talking up Theo in promo slots, paying him respects, bolstering his legacy. No thank you. But I'm having a baby, aren't I? That's a good thing, a wonderful thing. And I'll teach her not to behave like me, or teach him not to behave like Theo."

Molly nodded. Thinking of the future at a moment like this, refusing to reside in the past, was impressive and almost unfathomable to her.

"But how can you get past Theo?" she said, speaking slowly, her words swallowed up by the studio baffles as soon as they left her lips. "Don't you hate him? And doesn't that hate do something to you?"

Now Camilla finally took her hands. She stared into Molly's eyes. "No," she said, her precise performance now reinstated. "He was created by something in the world. He was bad, maybe, but he was a product of badness too. When everybody confirms to somebody like him that he's fundamentally in the right, that he's invulnerable..."

Molly shook her head. Whether this was true or not wasn't her concern. "What do we do about him?"

Perhaps Camilla sensed Molly's investment, her fight with the past. Perhaps she was less insightful, reacting only to Molly's use of 'we'.

She rose from her chair. "What can you do about a man like that?"

Molly was still sitting in the studio, facing Camilla's empty chair, when the door sighed open and Colin's red face appeared.

"Hey," she said. "How was the journey?"

Colin blew out his cheeks. His coat snagged on the door handle. He spun twice, trying to disentangle himself.

"You're drunk," Molly said.

He displayed only a momentary flash of shame. "I didn't have to come," he replied, swallowing a hiccup. "The money's not worth the harsh ship – hardship – you put me through."

She gave him a tight smile. "I'll go easy on you."

In the control room she ignored Colin's fumbling attempts to remove his coat and settle himself before the microphone. She brought up the collection of work tracks: the radio mic track, the environmental track, Colin's previous attempts to synthesise Theo's performance. She opened another bundled collection of files, to which she had dedicated far too much of her free time since the automated dialogue replacement sessions had begun. These were 'bed' tracks intended to act as background to various types of locations: *interior (close), interior (wide, warm), interior (cold), exterior (wide, open).* She had constructed them by isolating silences before, after or within Theo's dialogue, looping and combining silences to produce steady ambient tones. When the studio was empty she had returned to them again and again. She had played the recordings at home and in her car. Lacking the man himself, the silences would lend authenticity to the fake performance. Surely that was the only way to approach fidelity, to capture the memory, to capture *him*.

She selected each of the ambient tracks in turn and set them running all at once. *Interior, exterior, close, wide, warm, cold.*

Cold, cold, cold.

The sound washed over and around her from the speakers, making her gasp with its chill. She knew that there were no aberrations, no interruptions to the smooth flow of ambient sound, no clips, no murmurs of the crew. She could see the regular waveforms onscreen and yet—

Amidst the hum and the hiss she heard a distant cough. It was not only far away, it was muffled – by the backdrop, the heavy curtains, the many other bodies in the auditorium. It was not on the recording, this precipitant sound, and it was gone before it had begun and now she was there, back then, her hands pinned, her eyes wide and full of his looming face, her ears full of nothing.

In the silences she heard him.

And he was there. He was there, in the past and in the present, backstage and in the control room. He was in the recording and he was outside of it and he reeked with the confidence that he always would be.

"I have you in my sights," he breathed and the words were warm and sickly against her face.

No.

No.

What can you do about a man like that?

She held down the Control key and selected each of the ambient tracks, each of the silences full of threat.

Delete.

Are you sure?

OK.

OK.

She composed herself quicker than she had expected.

"I'll play you the production track and then you can dive right in, all right?" she said.

Colin eyed the ceiling as he listened to the playback. He coughed – a sound with no significance – and repeated, "You may have helped me, and you may be stranded, but I can't make your safe delivery my concern." He slurred the word 'stranded', hurried over the pause, missed out the word 'home'.

When he had finished he rubbed an already red eye and gazed up at the control room window. Cautiously, he asked, "How was that?"

Molly glanced at her screen, performing a cursory check of the waveform. She clicked Save. Without looking back up into the studio, she flashed a thumbs-up.

"Yeah," she said as she brought up the next line of dialogue. "That'll do just fine."

THE LONELY

Rich Hawkins

*

The voice was barely audible in the low hiss of the flame as the pot of milk slowly boiled on the gas hob.

"*She is the lamb.*"

Joyce had been staring out the kitchen window, towards a sky of stars above the murky lights of the town; upon hearing the voice she turned towards the cooker, and her face creased with slight confusion. She wet her lips from the glass of water in her hand then returned it to the worktop and leaned one side of her head towards the boiling pot, straining to listen. The voice was gone, but there remained a vague, wordless whispering that continued until she turned off the hob and all went to silence in the kitchen.

She poured the steaming milk into her Wonder Woman mug and shrugged, allowing herself a meek smile, before she switched off the light and returned to the living room to watch *I'm a Celebrity*.

She only turned back once to look at the darkened kitchen.

The milk frothed in her stomach as she lay in bed later that night, staring up at the ceiling, unblinking. She thought about work in the morning, and how she'd have to get through another day of anxiety, toil and clock-watching at the office. Joyce exhaled, rubbing her belly as gases and juices squirmed and popped within. The thudding footsteps and knockings of the tenants in the above flat and the insistent rain at the windows were constant reminders of her broken down life. She didn't even have a man, or a woman, to share her bed, and of all the thoughts to pester her at night, it was the realisation of loneliness that needled her the most and left her morose and sniffling in the dark.

In the morning, there was laughter in the walls as she tried to tune the radio on her bedside table. She turned it off and went downstairs to get ready for work. At least it was Friday.

The office smelled of bleach and bad breath. People flitted past Jane's desk without acknowledging her. She typed numbers on her computer and scrolled through digital files to check on invoices and receipts and manifests. She worked in silence. Every now and then she glanced at the digital clock nearby.

She flinched when someone gave an excited shriek from one of the adjacent cubicles. Her fingers paused at the keyboard. The monitor screen's pallid glow fell against her face. The scrape of a chair leg was followed by footsteps behind her. She didn't turn to see who it was, and eventually went back to work, falling into a practised method to shut out the office around her.

When the radiator on the nearby wall began ticking as the central heating kicked in, she thought she heard voices muttering wordlessly within its inner scrapings and toil.

She changed into jogging bottoms and an old sweatshirt after returning home from work. The walk up the stairs to her flat had been accompanied by the usual smells of urine and dampness, and from behind each apartment door she passed there had been a hushed silence, as though the tenants were playing a cruel game to perpetuate her loneliness. The shopping bags in her hands had knocked against her legs, irritating her to the point where she was gritting her teeth and stifling a frustrated growl.

Now, she sat on the sofa watching *Moulin Rouge* while picking with disinterest at a microwave dinner. A bottle of white wine was her companion for the night. She drank greedily while mouthing the lines of Nicole Kidman's character. Her timing was perfect between each mouthful of wine, as she imagined herself swept up in a great romance with a handsome stranger. And in her mind, it was her face on the television screen, playing the role of Satine, the cabaret actress and courtesan, the most beautiful of all, admired by all of Paris.

"Just a fairy tale," she whispered, and kept drinking.

Once the film was finished Joyce staggered to the window that looked out over the street below. She swayed until she placed one hand on the wall next to the window. Streetlights burned bright, too vivid for her timid eyes, and she lowered her head a fraction to peer down at the people heading out to bars, pubs and restaurants. Couples held hands. Some kissed and laughed, and their behaviour seemed exaggerated, as though they were aware of her looking down on them and wished to provoke her with senseless scenes of affection.

Joyce stepped away from the window and closed the curtains.

She woke in the night to the invasive drone of traffic from the main road. And in that background noise she heard other voices, all mixed together, like a party was being held in a flat on the top floor of the apartment building.

Saturday morning was full of rain, and she stayed in bed until midday hoping that her hangover would fade away. When the strain on her bladder became too uncomfortable, she stumbled out of bed with the duvet wrapped around her shoulders. After she was done in the bathroom, Joyce dressed in the previous night's clothes and switched the kettle on to make a cup of tea. She listened to the walls. A radio was playing in one of the surrounding flats. Background noise, garbled and faint. At least the party on the upper floor would have finished by now.

Joyce began to hum a low tune; it was the theme song of something from her childhood, now nameless and obscure and only remembered by those with a speciality for nostalgia. She stopped and listened, but there were no voices in the growl of the boiling kettle. She had just started to hum another song when she noticed the paltry shape of a deflated yellow balloon on the kitchen worktop. A party balloon all creased and shrivelled. Yellow was her favourite colour.

She picked up the balloon and stared at it for a moment then held it near her nose and sniffed, immediately grimacing at the combined smells of rubber, old perfume, and men's cologne.

She frowned, spoke in a whisper. "Where did you come from?"

After she dropped the balloon into the bin, Joyce checked the door of her flat and found it locked then did the same to the windows. All shut and locked. No one could have slipped inside her flat and left the balloon for her to find. She remembered the sounds from the party on the upper floor and sat down, folding her arms across her chest.

Her heart almost stopped when a burst of shrill laughter came from the adjacent flat.

Wrapping herself in a blanket on the sofa, she watched *Moulin Rouge* again, and increased the volume in an attempt to drown out the joyful voices blaring amidst the rattling pipes in the walls. But even as she tried not to listen she could hear specific words rise through the noise.

"...*succulent meat...warm...tender...we need it...*"

"*She is the lamb.*"

"*Can she hear us?*"

"*Is she listening?*"

"*We love her...*"

"*We love her so much.*"

Joyce kept her finger on the remote control's volume button until it couldn't go any higher and the neighbours started banging on the walls. Several angry voices displaced the sounds of the unknown party. A baby was crying. The dog in the apartment below barked and growled.

She fled from the flat, only pausing to hurriedly pull on her trainers and an old jacket.

Joyce stumbled through streets of uninterested people and grey buildings, pausing only when she glimpsed occasional figures dressed in frayed party gowns, crumpled tuxedos or tattered Hawaiian shirts lurking in nearby alleyways. The figures wore masquerade masks or had their faces painted to look like caricatures of animals. Mammalian grins upon pallid skin. Some held balloons that swayed in the breeze, while others clutched cocktails infested with tiny umbrellas. Two men dressed in drag, their faces lurid with smeared lipstick and white paint, used canes to beat upon the hide of a piñata that looked like a mangy dog. A little boy in a flat cap and a stained tuxedo pushed scraps of unknown meat from a bowl into his busy mouth. A thin female form wrapped in a feather boa of vivid red blew a kiss to Joyce then spread the stance of her legs to offer a glimpse of the fetid shadows beneath her ragged cocktail dress.

"She is the lamb."

Joyce kept moving. She heard the cheering and laughter in the noise of the wind and the droning traffic. She heard the sound of the celebrations spill through the streets. And when the sharp detonations of party poppers rose from within the noise of nearby roadworks, she cried out and threw her hands to her face.

Soaked through and trembling with cold and near-hysteria, she found refuge in the local park, huddling beneath a winter-worn oak of bare branches, where dead leaves and acorns rotted around her feet. The ground smelled of decomposition and fetid damp. She clung close to the gnarled trunk of the oak, glancing around the immediate area as a few people passed, either walking their dogs or strolling hand-in-hand. Some families walked together. None of the people wore masks or party clothes. None of them grinned at her with lurid faces. None of them revealed to her the inner folds of their lumpen bodies.

But even in the background noise of the town, the murmur of joyful voices and celebration rose to prominence. There was no respite.

And in her loneliness, she envied the other people of the world. She envied their comfort and shared warmth, their friendships and sex lives, their marriages and domestic drudgery. She hated them for their happiness and the dreams of their children.

"*Come find us*," a chorus of voices whispered in the cold breeze. "*Come and dance and laugh with us. You don't have to be alone.*"

Joyce sobbed into her hands. She didn't want to be alone.

When the light began to fade across the town and the streetlights blinked on beyond the park, Joyce rose from her crouching position at the foot of the oak and departed with trudging steps and trembling limbs.

She reached the edge of the park and halted at the dozen yellow balloons strung to the metal railings. Upon each balloon was written WE LOVE YOU, JOYCE in a child's handwriting.

A party horn had been left for her on a metal post. She

picked up the small object and unfurled the paper tube before letting it resume its curled shape. The yellow feather at the end of the tube tickled her nose.

When she put the plastic mouthpiece to her lips and blew, the comedic tooting sound returned to her memories of childhood and the loving embrace of her parents and friends. And for the first time in a long while she felt some solitary comfort, and smiled.

Joyce returned to the flat, which was dark save for the jaundiced light coming from beneath the door of her bedroom. Yellow balloons swayed in the dim corners. The scent of rich, old perfume made her feel giddy and weightless, and quickened her heart. The faint sounds of a party grew louder as she crept towards the bedroom. Honey-soft voices whispered her name and offered encouragement to her hesitant steps.

When she opened the door and stood wavering at the threshold, the sagging and wizened figures in antique dresses, gowns and threadbare tuxedos at the back of the room turned towards her with various grins and grimaces. Her bedroom was decorated with bunting, more yellow balloons, party banners and sepia photos of her as a little girl. The smell of perfume and cologne was strong enough to bring tears.

Vivid eyes regarded her from behind snouted masks. A short man honked through the bulb of his red nose. Faces seemed to crumple with the effort of joyful expressions. And they welcomed her with raised arms and busy mouths towards the centre of the room, where upon a long table an ornate silver platter tray lay prepared with trimmings of vegetables and pots of gravy and other sauces. She expected a steaming cut of meat, maybe beef or pork, but the lack of a main course did not trouble her. Plates and cutlery lined either side of the table. Dinner placings arranged for the discerning appetites of her new friends.

Liver-spotted hands of skin and bone reached forwards and prodded and pinched her flesh. A shrill voice spoke well of her rump and thighs. Some of the mouths that drifted close to her face cooed and gave shuddering sighs.

"*She is the lamb.*"

Joyce succumbed to their busy hands and was never lonely again.

A Shadow Flits

Carly Holmes

❋

The look on Helen's face was more curious than frightened. A blank bewilderment, a beseeching smile lurking behind the frown as she held the boy out to her husband. The nightlight glowed over the child's cheeks, shadows bunching in the pocket of his throat. "I heard a noise," she said, "and when I went to check he was on the floor. I can't wake him. Come on now Robbie, wake up, pumpkin." The hard kiss she pressed to her son's head nudged it sideways so that it swung down and dangled from his neck like a lampshade knocked askew from its stand. He let out a brief sharp grunt and a foot kicked once then was still.

Ed rushed them from bedroom to kitchen, wrapping them both in his arms, running so fast down the stairs he stumbled and barely caught himself before pitching them all to the bottom. Helen flailed towards the phone as he swept newspapers off the counter and upended the fruit bowl. "I'll drive, it'll be quicker," he told her, finding the car keys and hauling at her waist, spinning them all towards the door. She resisted for a moment, staring from him to Robbie, then the shell of her composure cracked and she started moaning, a low constant sound that was almost a hum until it began to rise in pitch, splintering on each indrawn breath.

Sat behind the wheel of the car Ed was suddenly terrified that he'd forgotten how to drive. He wanted to tell her to be quiet, to let him concentrate as he fumbled the gears from neutral to first and then back. The gaudy street lights made a bauble of Robbie's slack face in the rear-view mirror and he looked away, turned the key and reversed off the driveway.

Helen's keening became a scream once they were through the entrance doors and flooded with the harsh, welcome sounds of the hospital. They didn't need to call for help or grab at a passing sleeve, people were suddenly all around them, unwrapping Helen's fingers from Robbie's shoulders, pulling back her arms to extract the boy. Ed pressed his wife's face against his chest as they followed the march of white, muffling the force of her scream but still feeling its vibration tickle through his rib cage.

They were led into a cubicle and their son was placed on a bed while they huddled against the wall and watched parts of him disappear and reappear in the gaps between bodies and wheeled machines. A sock slithered from one of his feet, exposing the sole of a foot ingrained with the mud of that afternoon's splash-and-stomp through the park. Ed glanced at his wife; he'd promised her he'd given the boy a good bath before bed. But Helen was quiet now and largely unseeing, nestled into Ed's side, ducking and twisting her head to follow the flurry of movement. Ed tried to answer the questions she didn't seem to even hear but he couldn't remember Robbie's date of birth, what he'd eaten for dinner, whether he'd been anywhere new or had experienced any different routines recently. He was helpless, smiling idiotically at anyone who spoke to him, cringing when a machine squawked or a voice rose in urgency.

It was Helen who filled in the forms, finally, as Ed crouched at her side and held onto her ankles. The strength that had propelled him this far, bearing his family to this place of rescue, was puddled at his feet and he couldn't stand. Helen, now, was the one in control. So pale her face kept fading into the walls, Ed had to blink and narrow his gaze to bring her back into focus; the tick of her eyes as they swung from the papers on her lap, up to her son and then back down every few seconds, were the only things that animated her. They'd been moved to a room with a window and a small camp bed folded into a corner, grim signs of a long haul. The room had emptied of people at some point over the last hour or two and it was just the three of them for now. They'd been told to go home and collect some essentials, eat something, check Robbie's bedroom for anything that could shed light on his condition. Machines beeped in regular crescendos, strangely comforting. Ed found himself following the rhythms, tapping out their sound onto his knee with a finger. As long as the machines kept to this tune, didn't deviate in beat or tone, everything was going to be okay.

"He seems to be sleeping well," he said to Helen after

she'd put the papers aside and leaned back in her chair. She looked searchingly, almost quizzically, at him, then at Robbie. "He's not asleep, he's unconscious," she said. "I don't think he could wake up right now if he wanted to." Her voice was blunt and neutral, beyond fear. "I'm not leaving him for a second," she said. "Could you go home and get some things for us? I'll write a list. Robbie will need his other pyjamas and Teddy Two Face. He can't settle properly without it."

Ed shifted onto his knees and then carefully levered himself upright, testing his ability to stand. "What's wrong with him?" he asked. "What happened?" He walked over to his son and stared down at the tiny bulge he made under the sheet. So still, not even his eyelashes moved. "He was fine when I put him to bed." He leaned over to feel the faint stream of breath coming from Robbie's mouth, touched a finger to his cheek and trailed it lightly down to his chin. There was a smudge of something dark on the side of the boy's neck. He tried to rub it away and bent for a closer look. "Is that a bruise? It looks like a thumb print." He covered it with his own thumb for a second. It was small, too small to be his. "You must have grabbed him too hard when you picked him up."

Helen stood beside him and peered past his pointing finger. "I can't see anything. Of course I didn't grab him too hard." She dusted Robbie's neck with her fingertips and then sat on the bed and took his limp hand in both of hers, cradling it between her palms. She spoke over her shoulder. "There's nothing there, Ed. Please just go home and get the things we need." Turning back towards her son, she bowed her head low so that her hair swung down to curtain her face. The dark spill brushed Robbie's forehead, the tips settling there and giving the boy the look of a fringe. He'd be furious if he were awake, thought Ed. He hates being tickled like that. "I'll go home then," he said. "No need for a list, I know what to get."

In the kitchen he picked up the scattered apples and bananas and made himself a black coffee, drinking it stood by the window, staring out at the swing set on the back lawn. The recent winds had skewed one of the swing seats, twisting its chain so that it reared out at an angle. Helen had asked him only last week to retighten the bolts and check the whole thing over to make sure it was safe, but he'd forgotten to. If he knew where she'd tidied away the toolbox, he could do it right now.

Wandering away from the window, Ed poured another coffee and sat at the counter. If he could find a thermos flask he'd brew some more to take back to the hospital with him, something to keep them both awake. And he should make sandwiches, maybe even bag up the leftover rice salad. He meandered from kitchen to lounge to study, steeling himself to mount the stairs. The house felt like a stage set, its very familiarity and sameness rendering it alien to him. Lamps glowed from their perches on sideboards and tables, making monstrous shadows of the toy trucks and farmyard sets left out from the day's play session. Ed straightened a cushion on the armchair and picked up the novel Helen was currently reading. He left it by the door with her reading glasses, pleased with himself for his moment of thoughtfulness.

In Robbie's bedroom he pushed pyjamas and a couple

of picture books into a carrier bag, looked around for his son's teddy of the moment. The curtains were drawn and the window fastened shut. What had Helen said? She'd heard a noise and found him lying on the floor? There was nothing out of place, no signs of disturbance or distress other than the blankets that were usually neatly folded around Robbie (so neatly the poor child could barely roll over or raise his arms, Ed had always thought) trailed from the bed as if he'd clambered out in a hurry. Or fallen. Maybe he'd simply tumbled out and banged his head? He could be waking up right now across town, concussed but ultimately fine.

Ed remade the bed with clumsy concentration, folding back the top sheet the way Helen would, so that the patterned under-sheet gave a strip of bright colour. It was wonky and wrinkled and so, after fussing with it for a little longer, he gave up and tugged the pillow further down on the mattress to cover his efforts, smoothing the material and lining the edges up with the top corners of the head board. Then he ruined the whole effect by climbing onto the bed and pressing his face into the linen, trying to find Robbie in a whiff of talcum powder or a stray hair. He closed his eyes for a while and when he opened them again he didn't know what time it was and wondered if he'd napped. There was a blotch of something black blurred in his immediate vision, so close he thought at first that he had something caught in one of his eyes and pushed his fists into the sockets. The vigorous rubbing made a satisfyingly squelchy sound that Robbie would have loved.

Sitting up, Ed refocused. There was a dark smear

across the crease of the sheet, about the same size and shape as the one he'd seen on his son's neck earlier, but now he could tell it wasn't a thumb print. It had a delicate pattern, like a section of cobweb or widow's lace. Like the fretwork of shadows that he loved to watch flit through the curl of passion flowers that clung to the trellis by the front door. He assumed he must have wiped grease or coffee grounds or something, across the sheet when he folded it back. He'd better get new bedding sorted out before Robbie came home, definitely before Helen noticed.

He used the sleeve of his jumper to rub at the mark. There – gone, as if it never were. He checked his watch and hurried through the rest of the packing, adding three likely looking teddies to the pile and carrying everything downstairs. Back in the kitchen he made a couple of rushed sandwiches, tearing the bread with the butter knife and then adding too much ham to hold it all together. He ate one immediately, with sudden desperate hunger, but put the other in a paper bag for his wife. When he left the house he kept all the lamps glowing and switched a couple of the ceiling lights in the lounge and hall on for good measure. Neither of them would want to return to darkness.

Helen was asleep in a chair by Robbie's bedside when he got back to the hospital. Her slight torso was scissored half across the bottom of the bed, her legs splayed. She was inches from sliding off the chair. Ed watched her for a moment, lowering himself slowly from the knees to place the bags down. Even in sleep she was tense with shock and fear, her hands balled to hammer heads and her skin stretched and shiny from the tears she must have finally succumbed to. She jerked and opened her eyes when he put a hand on her shoulder, straightening with a moan of pain. "Why were you so long?" she asked. "They've taken more blood. More tests. He's still not woken up."

Ed kneaded her shoulder as he turned to look at his son. It was as if the last two hours hadn't passed, as if he'd never left the room. Robbie was exactly as he'd been; his shape under the blanket, his face on the pillow, identical and unchanged. It was only the unhurried rhythm of the beeping machines that indicated he was even alive. Ed stepped away from Helen and closer to the boy. No, not quite unchanged. The blemish on his neck had spread, darkness now mottling from just below his earlobe to the ridge of his collarbone and creeping round to the wisps of hair at the base of his skull. "Look at this," he said to Helen, reaching behind him to tug her arm and pull her to her feet. "What do they say about this? It has to be connected to what's wrong with him."

She leaned beside him, almost toppling onto the bed in her haste to see what he saw. Her frame was poised for action, straining to rush from the room with something vital to present to the doctors. A reason for all this and the possibility of a cure, right in front of them, the thing that would wake her son up and return him to her. "What?" she said urgently. "What? Show me."

"There. My god, it's all over his neck. That rash, or whatever it is. It was just a small patch earlier but now it's all over him. Is it meningitis?" Ed ran to the door and called out; a hoarse, unintelligible sound that brought a nurse striding towards them. "Show him, Helen," he said, waving the nurse into the room. "Show him the rash."

The nurse joined Helen by the bed and bent over Robbie. But Helen wasn't pointing out the mark, she was just standing there with her hands tucked into her armpits, looking at Ed with something close to rage on her face. The nurse, after a moment's examination, turned to him questioningly.

"There. Are you blind? It's right *there*." Ed jabbed at his son's neck roughly, scraping the skin slightly with a nail so that a tiny patch of scarlet bloomed through the black filigree of the rash. He took Robbie's chin in his palm and jerked his head to the side, the better to show them. Helen slapped his hand away, hissing something with such venom it scared him and he twitched away from her, stumbling back from the bed. "I'm sorry, I didn't mean to scratch him. But you must be able to see it."

The nurse stood between them and said something soothing, gently stroking Robbie's hair from his scalp. "I can't see any rash," he said, "but I'll make a note of it anyway. It could be useful." He darted a quick, kind glance at Ed and then shared a longer, more meaningful look with Helen. "You're both exhausted and scared. Why don't you try to rest for a few hours and save your strength? Shall I help you make up the camp bed?" He addressed this last solely to Ed, guiding him towards the corner of the room. Helen stayed at Robbie's side, standing guard over her son as if, Ed thought, she reckoned the boy needed the extra protection. He knew he was being handled by the pair of them, treated like some delusional fool, but he allowed himself to be led to the camp bed, allowed himself to be pressed down onto it once it had been unfolded, a firm hand on his shoulder patting him until he slumped into a shape of relaxation and turned his face to the wall.

After the nurse had left Ed twisted round and raised himself onto an elbow so that he could look at his wife. He watched her for a moment as she leaned over their son and murmured nonsense words to him. The anger had gone from her face, leaving it drawn and glassy, her hollowed cheeks and eye sockets floating like rotted lily pads on the surface of a pond. "Why are you pretending Robbie hasn't got those marks all over his neck?" he asked. "What are you trying to do to me? I don't understand."

She didn't look up at him, her attention focused entirely on Robbie. But she acknowledged the question with a quiet tut of frustration. There was silence in the room for a while, and then she sighed and spoke. "He hasn't got a rash, Ed. If he did, believe me I'd have seen it. The nurse would have seen it. I'm not saying you're making things up but you've got to stop muddying the waters. For Robbie's sake."

He reeled to her side and tried to reach past her, to touch his son. "God, it's all over him, how can you not see it?" he exclaimed. "It's spreading across his face now." Helen took his wrists and pushed him back. "Don't touch him," she said, "if you're just going to obsess about something that isn't there. You're not helping, Ed. None of this is helping. Go and lie down, get some sleep. Please." She held his wrists until he stepped back from the bed and gave a nod of compliance, then she released him and turned away, dismissing him entirely.

Ed lay on the bed and hauled the blanket viciously up to his chin, his fingers hooked around the hem, strangling the material. From his dark corner he watched the machines fizzing their signals in the pool of light around the boy's bed, rehearsing arguments and accusations to fire at Helen. What kind of mother could be so wilfully blind to her own child's suffering? He'd demand a meeting with the doctor in the morning, insist that someone took him seriously.

He woke briefly at some point in the pre-dawn, opened his eyes to see Helen stroking her fingers over the rash that had now crawled across Robbie's cheeks and was reaching to take his forehead. He blinked at the sight of her tracing the swirling patterns with her fingertips, closed his eyes and slept. When he woke again the window was creamy with early morning light. Helen wasn't in the room but he could hear her voice just outside the door. The tone of it, jarringly high-pitched and breathless, crisscrossing the low responses even as they rumbled on beneath her shrill questions, brought him to his feet.

"There's something wrong with his blood," she said to Ed when he joined her in the corridor. "They won't say what. They need to do more tests." She twisted her hands into the front of his shirt and tugged on it, shivering as she pressed herself close. Ed looked over her head to the doctor who'd delivered the news. "But that's good, isn't it? We're getting near to a diagnosis?"

As the doctor started to speak, doubtless about to

repeat the same bland statements he'd just made to Helen, she reared away from Ed and glared at him accusingly. "You shouldn't have left him. What if he woke up all alone?"

Ed waited until she'd gone back into Robbie's room, closing the door behind her with a firm, controlled snap that was as close to a slam as she would allow herself, and then turned to the doctor. "I'm sorry," he said. "She's quite overwrought." They both nodded, standing awkwardly together for a moment, then Ed stepped closer. "Can I ask you about the rash he's got? Can I show you?" He led the doctor to his son's bedside, ignoring Helen as if she wasn't present. "There." He waved a hand with a flourish that was almost theatrical.

With his eyes closed, his lips a thin, near bloodless, line, there was no part of Robbie's face that offered contrast or relief to the darkness that was now all over him, swarming from his hairline down to his throat and lower still, disappearing beneath the collar of his pyjama top. His skin was a web of shadow, an intricately patterned mask that seemed to shift the more Ed stared at it. He followed a patch dense as a storm cloud that flickered across Robbie's jawbone, focussing on it until it flattened and merged with the surrounding marks, and became part of the whole.

The doctor leaned over the boy. "Yes, I see," he said, peering at him. "He does have a slight rash. It doesn't look like anything more than mild dermatitis though, probably some contact irritation from the sheets. I really wouldn't worry about it." He straightened up and smiled soothingly, checking Robbie's chart as he backed away towards the door. "I'm afraid it's another day of tests today. It's going to be difficult for you both, so I suggest you get some food, take a shower, rest. Maybe even go home for a while." He turned briskly and left the room.

"Now will you please stop going on about the rash?" Helen's voice was weary, the harshness that had edged it previously now gone. Ed raised a hand to silence her. He couldn't speak. Stumbling to the chair at the other side of Robbie's bed he sank down and faced her. Between them his son lay unconscious, unbearably still but for the thing that rippled across his skin, shifting minutely almost between blinks to take more and more of him. Ed watched as Helen leaned down and pressed a line of kisses across the child's cheek, kisses that covered her lips with the same darkness. It caught in the corners of her mouth, spilling onto her chin, settling there to stain her pale flesh even as Ed turned away to the window so that he didn't have to look at her, at either of them, anymore. His fear was visceral, the healthy person's response to the plague victims and their leaking boils.

The teddies Ed had brought from home were the wrong ones. He was sent back to the house with a detailed description of the correct toy and a list of other instructions. Helen was worried about the potential fire hazard of leaving all the lamps permanently switched on and she wanted Robbie's bedclothes changed so that he'd have fresh ones ready for when he came home. As he left the hospital clutching his sheets of paper, Ed felt a surge of relief that was almost hysterical. He wanted to go for a drive, take the car for an aimless spin out of the city to a place green and open, and then walk for hours through a strange landscape, through woods and fields and alongside canals. He'd always tried to take Robbie for a walk through the local park at least once a week, coaxing the child to focus on the ground beneath his feet, see the insect creatures that scurried there. A long walk now would be a kind of homage to his son.

Instead, he drove straight back and let himself into the empty house. Though it had only been about eighteen hours the rooms had in them the dusty cling of abandonment. He moved dead air from kitchen to living room and back, opened windows and made toast. His mobile phone battery was low so he put it on charge and then consulted his list. It shouldn't be that hard to find the right teddy, Robbie must have had it in or near his bed if it was that important to him.

On his knees beside Robbie's bed, he peered beneath it. Nothing. Standing up, Ed surveyed the room. There were stuffed toys on the shelves and window sill but none of them matched the description he'd been given. He stripped the bed of its linen and then knelt by the over-spilling toy box in the corner of the room, pulling fistfuls of colouring books, action figures and plastic instruments out, spreading them across the carpet. Near the bottom, half-covered by a picture book, he spotted a fabric ear. That had to be it. He reached for the last few things, hauling the teddy and the book onto his lap.

The cover of the book, brittle and sticky from age, leered up at him from its place across his thighs. *A Shadow Flits*. He turned to the front page and saw his own name written there, his barely legible childhood scrawl covering the top corner. He turned more pages, following the story though he didn't need to read the words to remember how the tale progressed. A little boy, about Robbie's age, about the age he'd been when his own father had read it to him, lay terrorised in his bedroom night after night by malevolent patches of darkness that slunk out from behind the wardrobe and beneath the bed and peeped from around the curtains, waiting for him to close his eyes so that they could creep right up to him, could creep over him and into him and consume him.

Ed pushed the book away and covered his face. His father, taking some perverse pleasure from a small child's fear, had always stopped reading the book before the end, before the little boy in the story had been shown by his mother that these cruel monsters of the night were just shadows. *Look!* the picture book mother said. *See! It's just the nightlight making shadows appear. Let's switch the main light on. They're gone. Let's switch all the lights off. See how the shadows disappear!* The little boy, reassured, had been able to close his eyes and sleep. But Ed, for whom the story had always been paused at the point where the first shadows began to lick the boy's ears and nuzzle around his throat, had never known that moment of reassurance and relief. Only when his father died, when he was clearing out his home, did he read the book again and discover the ending.

Stumbling to his feet, Ed swept the book up and threw it across the room. He'd read it to Robbie at bedtime, again and again. He'd read it the way his own father had read it, echoing the trace of the generational sadistic impulse as if he had no choice, to stop at the same page and close the book with a snap. He couldn't explain why at the time, and he wouldn't be able to explain why now; it was just that there had been a unique twist of pleasure in witnessing the terror in Robbie's eyes as he shivered beneath his sheet and struggled to get a tiny hand free to clutch at Ed's sleeve. He used to beg not to be left alone, as Ed had done, and Ed had promised to stay but then had gone back downstairs and left Helen to deal with their sobbing son.

He'd only indulged that spiteful streak a few times, he thought, as he ran from the room. Surely only a few times. He'd stopped as soon as the self-disgust had overcome that bullying need to put his son through what he himself had been through. And within a week it was as if Robbie had forgotten completely about the flitting, hungry shadows. There had been no nightmares, no bed-wetting, nothing to suggest damage. Nothing apart from this sudden collapse and the darkness that was consuming the child. The darkness that was set on consuming Helen too.

His mobile phone was flashing, showing a voicemail message, when he reached the bottom of the stairs. He saw the missed calls on the screen and for a moment felt an urge to put it gently back down on the sideboard and just leave the house, sit in the garden for a couple of hours with a beer and watch the afternoon sunlight drift along the fence; stay safe and ignorant until the day disappeared entirely and the streetlights shed their garish glow across the bushes that bordered the property. He scooped the phone up and pressed the button before he could follow the impulse, steeling himself against the words that were stored up inside the little machine, waiting for him.

"He's had a fit, some kind of fit. His brain. They're trying to stabilise him now. Please come quickly."

The drive to the hospital, unlike the previous night's desperate plunge through the streets, was leisurely and slow. Ed idled through the neighbourhood he'd never really absorbed before now, noticing shady side-roads and alleyways he hadn't known were there. Skips and dustbins gaped with rubbish, hiding places for pouches of darkness. He crawled in first gear along sunny residential roads, ignoring the frustrated beeping of cars behind him, and sped through the murky spills that the trees and buildings cast over the tarmac, slowing again once he'd cleared their grasp. They were following him, he was sure of it. The shadows weren't satisfied with tattooing their claim over the faces of his son and wife, they wanted him too. Across the bonnet of the car they flickered and hunched, spraying like sundae sprinkles across the doors and windows.

After he'd pulled into the hospital carpark and found a space, Ed sat for a while and stared out at this new light and dark world. His mobile phone kept ringing but he didn't reach for it. As he left the vehicle he was careful to take an exaggeratedly wide step away from it, jerking himself up and out from his seat to avoid the vast clutch of shadow that waited beneath the car. He skipped and dodged across the carpark, sidling quickly through the door.

When he saw Helen, her face as inky as their son's had been, he couldn't bring himself to put his arms around her to comfort her. He sat on the other side of the empty bed, listening to her frantic description of what had happened. Her words looped and faded and rose in pitch, stuttering through the memory of the efforts made to bring the boy back to life. He stared at the place where the pillow met the mattress, its overhanging hem creating a thin sliver of shadow that writhed a little across the pristine sheet. He concentrated just on that cruel wedge of darkness until she finally stopped speaking and reached out a shaking hand to him, and even then he kept his head bowed and his fingers laced together in his lap, and he didn't look up.

The Butchery Tree

G. V. Anderson

❋

We gather on the heath to watch the red sun sink past the crown of spruce and birch. I'll not see its light again for months, nor my husband, Ges – winter always takes the clansmen to war. He stands apart from me, from us all, as a prince should, his hands clasped behind him. I resent the chill around my waist where a different, low-born man might wrap his arm.

Still, my front is warm: the sling that cuts into my shoulder is full of newborn baby. A boy. Blue veins lace his closed eyelids, his pupils roaming as he dreams. His father's coppery hair peeks out from beneath the swaddling hood.

Our first child, and the clan's pride.

Between my legs, I'm one big bruise.

Ges spares his son a smile before leading us home for the winter feast. I walk unaided, flanked by my handmaidens. As I pick my way over the hummocks, every step sends warm, stinging blood trickling down my thigh. I haven't moved so much since the birth and wonder if I've pulled my stitches. I press my mouth to the baby's fontanelle, firmer than I know I should. To the world, it must look like the gentlest kiss.

We climb the stairs to the hall where the rest of our clan waits. Inside, it's dark and close. Smoke from the spits hangs in the air, herbs burn thickly in the table fires, and plated joints of mutton glisten with a willow-honey glaze. Two hundred men, women and children are either sitting or serving, with mud-pawed hounds underfoot sniffing for scraps and fat dripping from the tables onto the floor where it cools and spreads, glutinous as lava. My stomach turns. As more people flow past me to take their seats, I mutter to Ges, "I must sit down."

"Not yet," he says, steering me to the dais. "I have a farewell gift for you."

He must see I need to rest, he must – my cheeks are clammy and my vision pops purple and orange – but his grip reminds me I have something to prove. Ges plucked me from obscurity, offered to make me his consort even as the mud of the grasslands dried between my toes, and the clan has watched me ever since, waiting for proof of my poor stock like a horseman watches a wild filly. I feel their eyes on me now, their whispers falling around my ears like thin snow, as Ges guides me to the high table.

It's bare, the grain unvarnished and rough. The wood gives off a ripe, decadent sort of stink like fruit on the turn. It's neither birch nor spruce. There's only one other tree on our land thick enough, old enough, to make such a table. I look at Ges in horror.

He grins and brings his fist down upon the grain like

a hammer striking an anvil. "I had it cut down for you," he said. "You need never fear it again."

※

It was called the butchery tree even before I was born. Goatherds did their culling there. Legend has it the last warriors left standing after a great battle met their deaths beneath the boughs. It grew in clay, and in summer blossomed red. No-one could agree what kind of tree it was. Some suggested rowan, but the trunk was all wrong: thick and veiny as a giant's cock.

I was six years old when Frodi strung me up in it by my wrists.

I remember him looking up at me from the ground, my toes swaying past his chin, my shoulders popping from their sockets. "Pretty," he'd said. "Pretty, pretty." His gums were too big for his mouth, and he had just a few flat teeth. I'd been scared of those teeth, and his unnatural bulk, for years. The boys went to him willingly. They dared each other closer thinking it made them look brave. Frodi had to snatch me; I was an afterthought. That's why I was merely hung before we were found. That's all he had time for after pulling the boys' innards out, leaving them to swing by their ankles, by their necks, their broken ribs clacking like wind chimes.

※

It's so typical of men to make trophies of what scares them, as if fear can be brought to heel. Ges's father was gored by a muskox, so Ges hunted it down and stuffed its head. He keeps it by the dais, using its tusks to rub mud off his boots. By turning the tree of my nightmares into something mundane, he thought to diminish it.

But my fear is subtler than that, and now it touches every aspect of my life. When I dine, the table creaks like old rope. I keep accounts, settle the season's last trade disputes and hold court wondering if its stench is native to the heartwood or an old stain I can't see. In the privacy of my rooms I nurse this baby, who clings to me always and cries for milk. His scalp has never quite lost the haemic tang of birth.

One of my handmaidens, Svala – little Svala, we call her, little bird – leans in to stroke his doughy cheek. Our bellies grew heavy together. Her daughter was born dead but her body hasn't caught up yet. "What a pretty young prince. What a pretty, pretty thing!"

"Take him," I finally say, loosening the sling and handing him over. Gods, what a weight he is!

He squalls in Svala's arms when she tries to feed him herself. "He's bloated, little bird – here." The other handmaidens take over, patting his back to wind him. One of them, Roslaug, shoots me dark glances as I tuck away my breast with its cracked and bleeding nipple. She hates me. She is the clan's highest-born daughter, the woman Ges was supposed to choose. It's a great slight that he looked elsewhere for a wife.

I press my palms to my sore back and stand in the doorway to the dais. By the light of fatty, sizzling candles, the clanswomen are hard at work, weaving and salt-packing, disciplining children, sharpening tools. In any other life, my hands would join theirs. In this one, it would be unseemly. So, I hover. I watch their industry.

Candles are fickle friends. The slightest gust and they gutter, hissing, making the shadows dance about. Such a gust chills me now and distorts all the faces in the hall. My eyes flick to the table.

Frodi watches me from the grain.

My eldest handmaiden, a God-witch called Hanna, appears at my side. She starts to tell me something about the child, some adorable thing he's done to entice me back, but then she notes my face, my shallow breath. "My lady?"

I point. "Do you not see...?"

But no, steady light is restored – it's not Frodi. I see now it's only the flaws in the wood, the knots and burls and chatoyant flares that take on the aspect of depth, a face. For a moment, I saw the bulge of his brow, the swell of his gummy cheek in the stress lines of that great old tree. I bring a hand to my forehead. Rope burns shine on my wrists. Hanna looks at them and quickly away.

"You need to rest," she says, chafing my upper arms through my sleeves.

"All I do is rest." And I'm sick of it. Like a foal, I was born on my feet and expected to walk. My family were goatherds who followed the annual thaw from heathland to hot spring and back. Musky oil from the bucks stained our hands; when Ges brought me here, I reeked. But I was proud of my living. We supplied the clan with milk, meat, and hides. My marriage to Ges grants them easy passage through his land from one grazing to the next, and I'm proud of that, too. What I'm not proud of are my hands now: smooth, nails long, clean. And how even in the winter, when I assume my husband's role, I only administrate by proxy.

I thought leaving my family behind and rising in the world would have given me more power, but instead I have less. As consort, I'm little more than a sow. A womb to make more princes and two teats with which to feed them.

And Roslaug envies that state? She'd be welcome to it.

Pretty. Pretty, pretty. I was rarely called so. I grew up on goats' milk, still frothing and warm, and salty, crumbling cheese. I grew up on fatty cuts and raw prunella. I ran my palms over the bucks' backs and slicked my dark hair out of my eyes. I was a wild thing, the wind splitting my cheeks and lips till they glowed scarlet. After being hung in the butchery tree I had bloody bracelets to match, and I refused to shy from men ever again: my gaze ground them down slowly like ice carves a fjord. It took Ges by surprise. Clanswomen look at their toes, except in winter.

He asked about me, the girl with irises pale as dew-frost, and someone would have told him – my story was well known. While his late father negotiated land boundaries between us goatherds and a neighbouring clan, Ges stole down to the butchery tree to find me. I often sat in its shadow when we passed by every spring, every autumn. I liked to remember the boys who died there. I liked to stab the bark with my knife.

"I'm told your name is Irja," he said.

"It means rain," I replied. I used to think it pathetic – a drizzle; a mist burned away by noon – until I watched storm-drops hitting the rocks around the hot springs. That kind of rain slices right through you.

The boundary talks lasted eight days, and I let Ges fuck me under the butchery tree on the sixth. I told him to pin me by the wrists, bound on my terms this time. My hands went numb, he gripped them so tight. Look at me, he said, and when he finished it was like he shuddered with cold.

❋

It's not Frodi's face, just random dark flecks, but I've seen it once so my eyes can't help picking it out again and again. As winter advances, we have to conserve our candles: the gloom deepens and reaches around us like little devils holding hands. In the dark, the lines of Frodi's face become firm and deliberate. There's a ridge that catches the light of the table fires, stark as the whites of his eyes.

I run my fingertip over it, tracing the shape for Hanna. She has a mole on her top lip. Lit from below, its shadow stretches up her cheek like a gash.

"It can't be by chance," I whisper. "It's just how I remember him, I swear to the Gods."

She wraps me in her arms from behind, cups my sagging belly with spotted hands. She smells of sleep-sweat and old furs.

"Tell me what he did."

I suck the bitter air until it burns my chest. I describe the boys, their positions as best I dare. The memory is so mangled by time, there are gaps: am I recalling truth, or the story I've always told myself? In the story, Frodi kills them one summer night, when the dark's so fleeting it swallows its own tail almost as soon as it's come. I remember a weak dawn bruising the sedge that grew between the roots, and my pensile feet.

"Human sacrifice is old, old worship."

God-magic? I know little of this. I turn and press my face into Hanna's shoulder.

"Perhaps it displeased the Gods so they trapped him inside the tree as punishment," she goes on, thinking aloud.

Frodi, trapped – alive? No – a strangled cry escapes me – no, I watched him die! The boys' families wanted to hang him. Mine wanted to feed his balls to the goats. Others thought he should be taken to the hot springs and drowned. In the end, they did a little of everything.

I'm shaking. Hanna calms me a little. God-magic is never literal, she says. Whatever lurks in the grain now is a shade, nothing more. But what if it's not just Frodi the Gods trapped, but a shade of every awful thing to happen beneath that tree? For I don't know what else that stink can be but blood and bowel, terror, tears and bile.

"I want it burned, Hanna."

She prises me off. "No, no," she murmurs, "who knows what protection the Gods placed upon it. It's a wonder it was cut down. And it was a gift from the prince. Think how that will look, my lady."

It's my table, I want to snap.

Hanna covers it instead, which I hate. I prefer to look a threat in the eye.

The clanswomen find it amusing. Winter has only tickled at us until now, feather-soft and playful. As the deep frost begins to bite, as the town's pathways harden and the livestock are brought in, they say I'm going mad. They say I'm soft because as a child I always spent winter at the hot springs. Perhaps they're right.

"Why do you cover the high table, my lady?"

Warm breath on my face one night, though *night* has ceased to mean anything without the sun cycling above us. I open my eyes. Little Svala lies facing me, her cheek resting on the back of her hand. My heart tugs at the sight of her – she's so young. The front of her tunic is damp with milk, smelling like my child should. Our feet are tangled for warmth. The cold's made us a litter of beasts.

"Because it's ugly." When did I become so craven? I should tell her not to go near it, but I don't like to scare her. I wonder if she sees through my lie.

She licks her lips. They parch and crack even before her tongue's finished. "Are you angry with the prince?"

No, I whisper; no, how can I be angry? It was a gift. Only – she's as open as a child and in the dark, secrets are easier spilled – only, I admit, sometimes, in the grain, I see a face I'd rather forget.

The child we made under the butchery tree came late. He turned over and over inside me for almost ten months and grew so big he cleaved me apart. Hanna induced him with hot baths and enemas, and by the time he finally clawed his way into the world, I'd lain in a drugged haze for hours. Sometimes I worry that's why I feel no bond: I wasn't conscious to welcome him.

I'm conscious now, and yet he still doesn't endear himself to me. He gorges until he's fit to pop, kneading painfully at my breast with his fists. Milk and slaver work up a pink froth around his mouth, gums chewing away at me. His lids hang open, showing white: in his glut, his eyes have rolled back.

"You must name him, my lady."

I glance up too late to catch the speaker. It's either Brigedda or Roslaug. Both are arctic beauties in their own right who'd have caught Ges's eye if I hadn't snagged it first. Perhaps they still will.

Svala rests her head on my shoulder, watching the baby feed. "The prince is supposed to name his heir."

"There wasn't time," says Roslaug. She has a strong jaw that juts when she's angry and she says *my lady* like she's striking flint with her tongue. Her touch was cool when she stitched me after the birth. I'm fond of her. "The naming takes at least a week and the men have been delayed long enough. My lady, I'll be frank" – more sparks – "there is ill feeling amongst the clanswomen. You cover the high table, you withdraw from the hall, and now you neglect our heir. He needs a *name*."

"So, it's neglect today?" I say. Fond I may be, but I also grow tired of being picked apart.

"Well, it could be ignorance." She smiles wickedly. I'm almost disappointed that she avoids my eye as she says, "What else should we expect from a goat girl?"

"Roslaug!" Svala has the grace to look shocked.

"Well, someone had to say it."

"At least eat with the clanswomen, my lady," adds Brigedda: peacemaker, chain-link, giant. As she leans forward, her hair clinks with metal cuttings and rings. "When you take supper in here, it's like you're too good for them."

I glare at her. "I won't sit at that table. I'd sooner burn it."

"If the prince made such a gift to me, I'm sure I'd be much more grateful. I should've opened *my* legs, too."

"*Roslaug!*" I've felt Svala's pulse grow frantic in her neck where it presses against my shoulder blade. Now she raises her head. "Neither of you are being fair. There's something foul about the grain, I've seen it myself."

I jerk my head. "What?"

She dips her head, cheeks pink. "I'm sorry, my lady. I was curious."

"Gods, what nonsense!" Roslaug flings off her furs and strides to the door. We all rise to follow her, though I hang back and hate myself for it. I could command her to stop, to shut up and sit down. My voice was never stoppered before. Yet now that I need it, when she's bursting onto the dais where Hanna holds court in my place, I'm choking—

—she grabs handfuls of cloth—

—everyone's watching—

Clanswomen gasp and mutter, their layered voices pitter-pattering into *pretty, pretty, pretty*. Children crane for a look.

Gods, he's there. He's still there.

He's not alone.

To them, it's faces. Just the semblance of faces, stamped at random. Shocking enough, but lacking the sickening punch of recognition that brings me to my knees. Frodi's as clear to me as a brand, and then there's the others, the boys...

Suddenly my wrists are bearing my six-year-old weight again. I'm turning my head towards the last boy alive. His breath's iron. Past his chin, everything's crimson and mauve. I don't look. I don't realise until much later that Frodi must be gutting him lovingly, carefully.

I call his name but the boy's fading, too far gone to cry.

We mark every change. The faces distort according to direction and light, shifting in the time it takes to walk from one end of the table to the other. Frodi's eyes always follow us. His mouth bends into a smile within two hours, which slowly widens when the children come forward. We keep them away after that.

"Cover it up!" Roslaug says.

"No." I stop Hanna as she reaches for the cloth. "We can't ignore it. We know it can spread."

Every clanswoman, old and young, court and common, is given the chance to speak, and most agree it should be burned despite Hanna's warnings. They don't look to me to pass sentence. They've weathered many winters without me, and will weather many more; my opinion alone doesn't signify.

"Do it now!" someone cries.

"Take it outside!"

I won't touch the bare wood. I wrap my hands in cloth before I grab one end. Brigedda takes the other. With Hanna chanting behind us, we haul it outside. The stairs are submerged by snow packed under a hard film of ice, treacherous in the dark, so we fling the table down the slope where it lands amidst the outbuildings with an ear-splitting crack.

As the women fetch fuel, I unwrap my shaking hands and thrust them into the snow. The table was so perversely heavy, the cloth's weave has imprinted on my fingers. My teeth ache in the cold.

We coat the table with pine resin and Brigedda sets it ablaze. The sudden heat sucks the air right out of my throat. Everyone stays to watch until the black smoke makes it hard to breathe, then most retreat inside. The thing is done, they murmur. Svala goes to tend my crying baby. Only Hanna, Brigedda and Roslaug stand guard with me.

I scoop up handfuls of snow and press them to my burning face. After two thousand heartbeats, the table's blackened but unbroken; the squeal of splitting wood sounds like high-pitched laughter. Inside, my son is still screaming.

"Something's wrong," I whisper.

Hanna grabs me. "Gods help us!"

In the conflagration's heart, the wood bends like hot metal. A table leg, now more of a tendril, gropes at the melting slush. Finding no purchase, it gouges into the frozen earth beneath. Hooks in deep. Starts dragging its bulk towards me.

Brigedda keeps an axe in her belt. I snatch it, slide down the ice to meet what's left of the butchery tree, and land blow after blow. It's a small axe, I wield it one-handed, but the head is stout: each swing whistles. Burning resin splatters my arms and face. Flames lick my feet.

When I'm done, the table's pulp.

It's Hanna who pulls me away, presses me to her breast, and soothes me like I'm a child. Over her shoulder I see the clanswomen emerging, drawn by the noise, and Brigedda and Roslaug pointing to me, mouthing words I can't hear. The roar of the fire and my own pulsing blood have left a thick ringing in my ears.

Hanna's saying something. She's tugging my arm. I look down. I'm still holding the axe. My hand's clamped round the handle. The head drips dark resin like blood.

The clan's sheep are clever beasts. They balk at the sight of me, and they bleat all hours of the long night. Hanna supposes it's the liniment she used to treat my burns that they dislike.

The clanswomen always corral them into one corner of the hall before we sleep. I bury my hands into their waxy fleeces, grasp them by the ribs and shunt them along. They tremble at my touch. My palms emerge greasy, olid. At first, I wipe them clean on my trousers, but my hair gets in the way so much that I end up raking the wool-gloss through it instead.

"My lady?"

I glance up, my hands at my nape.

Svala bites her lip. "The young prince is hungry."

"Then nurse him."

"He won't latch properly." She looks down, almost crying. "I'm sorry, my lady."

I leave the women to their herding and follow Svala back to my rooms. The baby is growing quickly now. A plump little pear of a thing. He feeds without end and refuses any nipple but mine, though they're scabbed. Suppurating. I grit my teeth as he sucks.

"Ah!" I gasp suddenly, sucking air myself. I pull him off and poke a finger into his mouth. He has two hard teeth breaking through his bottom gum. I frown. He's barely four months old – too young for teeth, surely? I ask Svala but she's no wiser.

I peel back his lips to look at them. They are flat. Blunt. Slabs of enamel.

Frodi's teeth.

I don't stop to think – I fling him off me. Svala's shocked cry hits me like a dash of cold water. He lands by her feet, swaddling trailing loose. He doesn't cry... Oh Gods, why doesn't he cry? Have I broken his neck? We both reach for him, holding our breath, but he moves first.

With his arms, he starts to haul himself back to me. As he slips out of one shadow and into the next, I see his cutting smile. The swollen gum bulges against his lip. He clicks his tongue against his palate. A wet rhythm, *pretty, pretty, pretty*, like Ges pumping away at me under the boughs of the butchery tree. Once he's crawled free of the swaddling, he gets to his feet and walks on legs still bowed from the womb.

The axe is never far from me now; I keep it under my

bed. I lunge for it, pushing Svala away to safety. The fruit of that blasted tree pivots to chase me, but he's waddling on crude legs. He barely takes a step before I'm hacking at his head.

He bursts like a boil. All that milk in him, all that sap.

His bones, though: they splinter.

Roslaug's coup was effortless. No-one else witnessed the child walk, and precious few stayed to see the table burn. Hanna believed me, I think. She saw the body when I was done – the fibrous bone, the sticky resin soaking into the rug – but no-one had the stomach to corroborate her testimony, so it counted for nothing. And poor Svala. In her confusion and grief, she helped condemn me. I fled before facing my sentence.

I linger just long enough to see a dirty smear of men appear at the same time as the sun, towing the spoils of war behind them. They don't know it yet, but there's another war to fight at home. I pray Hanna will get the chance to explain everything to my husband before they kill him, for if Frodi can jump from tree to child, why not child to parent?

I turn to the wilds, relishing the cold. The horizon's as light as lapis lazuli. No longer someone's daughter nor wife – free, and yet not quite myself, whoever that may be – I am set loose upon the coming spring.

✳ ✳ ✳

The Lens of Dying

Charlotte Bond

*

"Three days," Dean murmured as he looked in the mirror. He dragged the razor smoothly across his cheek. "Three days and hands still as steady as ever."

He grinned. Yesterday, it had been two days after his seventy-sixth birthday and his hands hadn't shaken as he'd shaved, or eaten his eggs, or opened his front door. They weren't shaking today. They wouldn't shake tomorrow. He'd bet they wouldn't be shaking three hundred and sixty-six days after his birthday either.

He finished, splashed his face with water and reached for the towel by the sink. As he patted his skin dry, he looked in the mirror and saw someone standing behind him in the bathroom doorway. Himself, aged nine, dressed in a dark blue hoodie.

Dean spun round, his heart hammering. There was only his old dressing gown hanging on the door. He willed himself to turn and look in the mirror again. He fully expected to see that small, pale face staring back at him.

If he squinted hard, he could see how his dressing gown might look like a person. He could almost see how a trick of the light might make it appear there was a face in the shadows of the hood.

Dean hung the towel back on the rail. As he left the bathroom, he grabbed the gown and tossed it into the laundry basket. The touch of the towelling made him shudder.

He made himself some instant coffee, scraping the bottom of the jar for the last granules. He held a slice of bread, his hand hovering over the toaster before he decided his stomach was too unsettled to eat.

He didn't bother cleaning his teeth after drinking his coffee. That would mean going back in the bathroom.

Instead, he headed for the front door. After his shock, he needed some fresh air and space. The air inside the house felt stale, and the walls pressed too close.

As he passed the bookshelf in his hallway, he ran his fingers along the spines of the books there. The ritual brought him a sense of calm.

I'm not like them. They were sick. I'm sane.

And I ration myself. I am controlled.

As he was unlocking the front door, there was a knock on it. He froze, his hand gripping the knob. There was something about the knock, the weakness of it, perhaps, that made him certain it had been a child.

With a sudden rage at his own fear, he wrenched the door opened and bellowed, "What?"

An empty step confronted him. A woman walking her dog on the other side of the road glanced over, then hurried on.

He stared up and down the otherwise empty street before stepping out and locking the door behind him.

Instead of refreshing him, the fresh air chilled him. It still had the sharpness of winter in it. He sensed blurred movements everywhere, and they made him uneasy. A cloud passing in front of the sun made what looked like a child's shadow race across the pavement.

The fluttered edge of a poster on a telegraph pole looked like hair blowing in the breeze as someone tried to hide.

He glanced at the betting shop as he passed. It was a luxury he allowed himself once a week – and he'd treated himself this week, on his birthday. Nevertheless, he paused and fingered the fiver in his pocket.

Just one little bet. That'd be alright, wouldn't it? Just to take my mind off things.

He'd half turned towards it before he realised what he'd been doing. He forced himself to turn away. Control. Always control. Never overindulge. It was that kind of thing that got you caught.

He saw no more phantom movements, but when the bright yellow sign of the corner shop came into view, Dean's pace quickened. The moment he stepped over the threshold, he felt a shiver of relief go down his spine.

He grabbed a jar of coffee and went to pay for it. Behind the counter was a spotty youth who smiled as Dean approached. Dean tried not to grimace at the sight of crooked teeth.

As the kid handed over the change, he frowned and said, "You alright, mister?"

"Yes? Why?"

"Your hands are shaking."

Dean snatched his change and dug his hands into his pocket. "Don't be rude to your elders, you little brat."

The boy's pale skin went waxen. "Yes, sir. Sorry, sir."

Dean turned away, furious.

Useless kid. All kids are stupid at that age. Too lippy, too full of themselves. They're much better when they're younger. Too bad they have to lose their beauty and their innocence as they get older and turn into pimpled freaks like that one.

Dean marched outside and down the road, anger driving him. He could feel his rebellious body trembling, making him even angrier. He stopped and leaned against a wall. What movement there was on the street around him was mundane and expected. There were no more phantoms.

He took a deep breath, held it, let it out. He mentally conjured up his happy place: a small mound in a wood, covered with leaves and dead sticks so no one would see how it was different to the rest of the ground.

As he walked home, he turned the image over in his mind, examining it from every delicious angle. Then he thought of another grave, and another. The memories kept him warm and calmed his shaking limbs.

Lost in nostalgia, Dean decided to head in through his back door. He wanted to look at the apple tree. Burying her beneath it had been impulsive and terribly risky, but over the years he'd got so much pleasure from knowing she was down there. Many times, he'd stood beneath the tree and thought about her perfect little body beneath his feet. He recalled how the soil had covered up her lovely face, sealing it forever from the cruelties of the world.

He stood for a while beneath the branches. The buds were just starting to show themselves after the winter. "Beauty is in the eye of the beholder, Alison," he murmured, "and you'll always be remembered as beautiful."

As he turned to go back indoors, his shoe came down on something hard and thin. On reflex, he lifted his foot and saw three small fingers sticking out of the dirt.

Dean cried out and tried to back away, but he tripped over the hose he'd left coiled up on the grass last summer. He crashed to the ground. Pain exploded in his coccyx, shooting all the way up his back. The palms of his hands stung where they'd taken the impact of his fall.

Reflexive tears of pain filled his eyes. He scrubbed them away and stared at the dirt-covered fingers. One of them twitched, jerking upwards. Dean whimpered and scrabbled backwards.

It's impossible. It's impossible. It's—

"Mr. Simms? Are you alright? Let me help you up." Dean's neighbour, Cindy, came into the garden. Before she could reach him, panic gave him the strength to struggle to his feet and plant himself between her and the apple tree.

"Don't look! Don't go near it!" he said frantically. He waved his hands, trying to distract her from the accusatory fingers pushing their way through his lawn.

"What happened? Did you trip over those roots? They're a hazard. I'll get Matt to pop round later, dig them up for you. You want to be careful they haven't got into the foundations of your garage as well."

The tight knot in Dean's chest loosened a little. He

looked behind him. What he had thought to be fingers were, as she had said, exposed tree roots. The white patches he'd taken for fingernails were scuffs he'd made with his shoe, revealing the lighter flesh underneath.

It wasn't Alison after all.

A manic laugh exploded from between his lips. He clamped his hands over his mouth. His body shook with contained hysterical laughter.

When he saw Cindy staring at him with intense concern and a little fear, his laughter melted away. He coughed into his hand several times, trying to pass off his moment of mania as just a weakness of the lungs.

"Thank you, but there's no need to bother your husband. I've got a gardener I can call. He's the son of a friend of mine." The lies came easily, as they always had.

"Well, if you're sure. Can I at least help you inside?"

"I'll be fine. You'd best be getting along. What about the baby?"

"Oh, she's just round the corner, in her pushchair. She's not really a baby anymore. Would you like to say hello?"

Dean didn't, but it seemed that agreeing would get her off his property faster, so he followed her, limping a little.

He'd been expecting a wrinkled thing with drool on its chin. Instead, he saw a perfect little human being in a pink dress with small pink shoes and adorable white socks with frills at the top.

So beautiful. Almost the right age...

"She's a delight," he said, giving a practised smile as he forced all other thoughts from his head. He couldn't risk Cindy reading them in his face. She still wore her wary look from earlier.

"I'd better fix her lunch though. If you're sure you don't—"

"I'm perfectly fine, and so lucky to have neighbours as caring as you. I'm sure you must be an excellent mother to young, er," he faltered, her name escaping him, "to this little mite here."

Cindy blushed a little. "That's kind of you to say."

Flattery, Dean knew, was the best distraction there was.

Dean excused himself and went inside. He stood before his bookcase and gazed at its contents. He knew the titles so well, he could recite them with his eyes closed.

Criminal Shadows.

The Evil Within.

One Of Your Own.

Whoever Fights Monsters.

And so many more.

He knew all the names, the details, the final tallies. He lovingly stroked a spine and recited the details in his head.

Ted Bundy. Thirty or more. Kept severed heads. Had necrophiliac tendencies, despite being such a nice young man.

I find nothing remotely attractive about the dead, but I am a nice man. That's got to count.

Gacy. Thirty or more, but with sexual assault and torture this time.

I don't torture. I make it quick and painless. And I never had as many as him.

His finger moved on to another book.

Dahmer. Seventeen. There was necrophilia there too, and cannibalism.

Why would you spoil perfection with such a disgusting habit?

Another book under his fingertips.

Ed Gein. Just two confirmed, but all that shit in his house, that was sick.

I'm not sick, I'm sane. That's got to count.

Harold Shipman. Two-hundred and forty.

I'm not even close. Definitely not on his level.

Peter Sutcliffe. The Yorkshire Ripper. He prayed on prostitutes.

They had it coming if you ask me. What kind of nice girl gets into that kind of game?

I only deal with nice girls and boys. After they've spent time with me, their beauty remains eternal.

I'm a preserver of beauty. That's got to count for something.

Feeling infinitely calmer, Dean went to make himself a cup of coffee. He carried his drink into the living room, studiously ignoring how the liquid splashed over the edge onto his fingers, almost as if his hands were shaking.

He sat down and turned on the TV. It was permanently tuned to a channel that boasted endless reruns of cookery programmes, DIY shows, and garden redesigns. Not even moving from the sofa, Dean could visit the Norfolk Broads or the south of France and gain detailed insight into the lives of others – all the while safe in the knowledge that his life was hidden. Television was a voyeur's best invention.

When six o'clock came, Dean stood up and stretched his stiff muscles. He limped into the kitchen, his injury from earlier still paining him. He stared out of the window for quite some time, until he was sure that the exposed roots were still just that, and not fingers clawing their way up to the air.

He emptied a tin of ravioli into a saucepan and heated it up. He buttered some bread, pulled bits of mould off the crust and then set it all on a tray to take next door. He ate his meal while watching a small London flat be turned into a fairy tale kingdom for an eight-year-old girl and her five-year-old sister. Upon seeing the magic the TV team had worked on her daughters' bedroom, the mother burst into joyous tears. They weren't the kind of tears that Dean relished, but he felt his heart speed up all the same.

Careful now. Too excited and you'll not sleep tonight.

He took his plate out to the kitchen and pulled open the drawer where he kept his cigarettes. He stared in horror at the empty packet.

What the hell? A frantic search turned up no other packets, empty or otherwise. *I can't have run out. I always buy another packet when there's two left. I always do.*

A thought tugged at the edges of his brain. *Wasn't this one of the signs of getting old?*

Dean slammed the drawer shut and stood there, breathing heavily.

No, I'm only seventy-six. That's nothing in today's world.

My feet are not at the edge of the grave. He looked down at his slippers, just to check. Below their smooth soles was the same, familiar grubby linoleum.

His heart was now racing with trepidation rather than excitement. He drew deep, steadying breaths as he stared out of the window, into the darkening world beyond. His face was a pale oval superimposed on the gloom without.

A reflected movement over his shoulder drew his eye. His younger self stood in the doorway, hood up, eyes gleaming. Dean spun round with a scream, but there was no one there. He glanced back at the window, searching for what had caused such a mirage, but there was nothing that could possibly account for it.

Hurriedly, he slipped on his coat and shoes before heading for the front door. He was halfway down the hallway when the headlights of a car shone through the side window next to his front door. It made an uneven circle of light race across the wall. Dean thought about his own, pale reflected face in the glass and gave a nervous laugh.

I'm spooking myself now. It was just a light on the wall, not a face.

Five minutes later saw him back at the counter of the shop, buying a packet of cigarettes. The pimply youth was gone, to be replaced by a sour-faced woman.

"They'll kill you, you know," the woman said.

Dean felt an unnatural fear rush through him, and he snapped, "It's the only vice I enjoy. It's not too much to ask for one after my supper, is it?"

She gave him a withering look, but he shrugged it off and left. Normally, he allowed himself only two a day – one after supper, one before bed. But after the day he'd had, Dean decided he'd treat himself and have one on the way home as well.

To calm my nerves.

The street was mostly empty. He paused beneath a lamppost to light his cigarette. It took him several attempts. He told himself the flame in his fingers shivered because it got caught in a breeze.

As he took a draw, he caught sight of a face in a car window. A young boy was looking out, straight at Dean, his face close to the glass.

Dean stared back, his shoulders tensing. The cigarette tumbled from his numb fingers. He looked down, briefly, at where it smouldered on the floor. When he looked back up, he expected the child's face to have vanished or to have resolved itself into something more comprehensible, but it was still there. He looked beautiful and oddly familiar.

A shaky breath escaped Dean's lips as he walked forward, drawn as if by an invisible thread. He expected the boy to back away as he approached the car, but the lad just sat there, staring up at him with mismatched irises – one blue, one brown.

Just like Cody, he thought.

In one terrible, heart-juddering moment, three things became crystal clear to Dean. Firstly, that the boy in the car didn't *look* like Cody Bellweather, he *was* Cody Bellweather, a boy dead nearly seven decades. The second thing was that, although Dean's own breath plumed on the cold air, there was no mist on the glass before the boy's lips. And finally, Dean could see his own haggard face reflected in those beautiful mismatched eyes.

Dean stepped away from the car, shaking. His throat

tightened so much that his breath wheezed. The boy in the car lifted a hand to the window. The skin was bloated and white. Bones showed through the ragged fingertips as if the flesh on them had been gnawed away.

Dean turned and ran. Around him, shadows seemed to lurch to life, phantom limbs reaching for him.

When he got to his house, he took one look at the front door, steeped in shadows, and ran around the back.

It's fine. I didn't lock it. It'll be quicker going in this way.

The moment he put his hand on the handle of the back door, he was certain that he *had* locked it, even though moments ago he felt equally sure he hadn't. An image flashed through his mind of him, weeping, clinging to the door, as the shadows crept across his lawn to consume him. But the door opened, and he stumbled inside.

Tears of relief ran down his cheeks as he fumbled to turn the key in the lock. His hands were noticeably shaking now, but he didn't care anymore.

As he stepped away from the door, he looked into his garden. A neighbour's security light threw enough illumination onto the lawn to reveal a pale arm sticking out of the ground beneath the apple tree. The grass around it heaved as something tried to return to the light and air.

Dean's legs were so weak he was barely able to walk in a straight line through his own kitchen. He careened from counter to table, banging his hip painfully on the edge of the door before reaching the hallway. He grabbed the bookcase for support, but even the feel of the books beneath his fingertips brought him no comfort.

Once in the living room, he closed the door then backed away. His legs hit the arm of the sofa so that he fell, sprawling backwards onto the cushions. He lay there, panting, staring at the door, and trying to keep quiet.

He listened for the sound of claws or exposed bone scraping along wood as Alison tried to get in. But all was silent.

The room was warm. He was exhausted. As his terror ebbed, his eyes closed.

Dean started awake, shivering. Even though he could only see the ceiling above him, he knew instantly that something around him was different. He listened, wondering if a sound had awoken him.

It came to him: the light was different. When he'd stumbled in here, the room had been filled with warm lamplight. Now the light was white and stark and coming from the door – the door which now stood wide open.

A small figure stepped into the rectangle of light. Even though it was in silhouette, Dean knew who it was. The figure moved towards the sofa. Dean stuffed his hands into his mouth, trying to push the whimpers back down his throat as his own nine-year-old face stared down at him.

"We've come to take payment," the boy said.

"We? Who's we? What payment? I don't owe anybody anything."

The boy cocked his head. His look was one of pity. "Which question do you want me to answer first, old man?"

"Get out," Dean snapped. He could feel his fear

morphing into anger, and he embraced the change. Anything was better than the cold terror that had paralysed his limbs. He struggled to sit up and said again, more forcefully, "Get out!"

The boy glanced over his shoulder. The bookcase was a hulking shadow in the unnatural light.

"You read all about them, didn't you? You read about their lives, compared them with your own, and made sure there were just enough differences."

"Don't be stupid. You can't know that." Dean's voice shook as badly as his hands.

"I'm you. I know everything that you know."

"I'm seventy-six. You're, what? Nine? How could you possibly know everything that I know?"

"You should know exactly how old I am. I'm nine years, six months and three days exactly."

Bitter saliva filled Dean's mouth. "You're from *that* day then?"

"Don't you recognise me?" The boy lifted his arms to take in the whole room. "Don't you recognise *us*?"

Dean tore his gaze away from his younger self and looked around him. The shadows were undulating, taking on form. Some were bulging as nightmare creatures fought their way out.

A groan escaped Dean's lips as children emerged from everywhere, crawling towards him. He didn't need to count the twisted, grotesque figures. He knew exactly how many there were. Twenty-nine. Almost – but, crucially, not quite – as many as Bundy or Gacy.

Dean pushed himself as far as he could into the sofa, wishing it would swallow him and spirit him away from the ghastly children. Their beauty had not been preserved by his actions but had been leeched away. Perfect pink skin was now smeared with mud or was grey and hanging off in ribbons. Bright red blood covered the shoulder of one girl whose throat he'd cut. The boy standing next to her was drenched in black ichor from a stomach wound. He knew each of their names and remembered each of their deaths in perfect clarity, but he could not reconcile the monsters he saw before him with the angels he put in the ground.

"Why are they so hideous? They were supposed to stay beautiful."

"Beauty is a living thing. The moment you took their life, you took that away from them. If they're beautiful anywhere, it is only in your mind, where you revisit them over and over. Their real beauty was eaten up by the earth and the worms in whatever shithole you chose to bury them in."

A figure stepped up behind Dean's younger self, his mismatched eyes fixing the old man with a stare. Dean forgot all the other children closing in on him. For Dean Simms, seventy-six, the only thing that existed in the world was the beautiful, broken face of Cody Bellweather.

"It wasn't me," Dean whispered. "It was the others. I just watched. It wasn't me. It wasn't even my carrier bag."

"It must have been you" said his younger self, "or else we wouldn't be here."

"I don't understand," Dean said, his words breaking into a sob.

Cody leaned forward. His wondrous face was degrading even as Dean watched. But the corruption didn't reach his eyes, which remained as perfect as the day they'd buried him in the woods. And Dean could see the face of his nine-year-old self reflected in them.

"Can you see yourself? See me? Cody died that day, and you were the last thing he saw. The lens of the dying is a powerful thing. They say the last thing a dying person sees is captured in their eyes, like a photograph. As he died, Cody sucked part of your soul right out of you. You walked away from his grave, and you left part of yourself – me – behind, and we've been following you ever since."

Cody stepped back, releasing Dean from whatever hypnotism had paralysed him. It was only then that the old man realised the other children were pressed close around the sofa. They stood as silent sentinels, looking down at him.

He looked back at the doorway, hoping to appeal to himself, or to Cody, to end this nightmare. The light from beyond the room was no longer harsh and white, but the gentle glow of summer sun. His bookcase was now a towering oak. The bannisters of his stairs had morphed into young, willowy trees.

As his jaw dropped open, the children around him leaned over him. He didn't have the chance to try and ward them off before he felt their cold hands on him. His clothes were irrelevant to them. They reached through fabric, skin, and bone into the centre of him.

Innumerable small fingers squeezed his heart and tightened around his lungs so that he couldn't breathe. His eyes lost focus. There was a rectangle of light above him while around him was loose, dark earth. The part of him that wasn't shrieking in pain knew that he was in his own grave, or perhaps Cody's.

A silhouette appeared, blocking out some of the light. For one brief, wonderful moment, he thought it might be a paramedic come to help him. Then the figure shifted, and the sunlight revealed his own youthful face from a summer's day seven decades ago.

Yet even with the pain filling up his body, Dean could see that the face looking down wasn't the face of the boy he'd been talking to. There was a brief hint of that sad face in the lines of the eyes and the slight twitch of the mouth, then it was gone, sucked away. The face that looked down at him after that was the face he'd seen in the mirror growing up. It was filled with a secret joy and a twisted curiosity about the dying thing in front of it.

He remembered how it had felt to be standing over Cody, to watch the plastic bag they'd tied around his head go in and out, moving rapidly at first then less and less. His memories were so strong that it almost felt as if he was seeing two things at once: what he saw as a boy, and what Cody saw while Dean and his friends watched him die.

The duality of it all – being the observed and the observer – made his head spin. Darkness crowded around the face before him but didn't blot it out completely.

Panic coursed through Dean as the face came closer, looking right into his eyes as he struggled to breathe. The lips hovering before his face formed words. Dean couldn't hear them with the sound of blood pounding in his ears, but he knew what the boy said. It's what he said all those years ago.

"Well, look at that."

His body felt hot and cold at the same time. His arms became too heavy to lift. It was too exhausting even to breathe.

He stopped hearing the blood in his ears. He ceased feeling the hard press of earth into his back. He couldn't smell the rotting children around him, or the scent of summer flowers that filled the air that day they'd killed Cody.

For a fleeting moment, he wondered about the friends who'd been with him when Cody died. He couldn't remember their names, not the way he could remember the names of all the children. He wondered if Cody would visit his friends too. Perhaps, but then, their face wasn't burned onto the boy's soul.

Dean's senses started to desert him, and he welcomed it. He just wanted everything to be over.

But even when he couldn't feel, or hear, or talk, he could still see. He could see a terrible black shape surrounded by light. He could see lips moving, expressing wonder, and eyes burning with the fierce joy that had powered him the rest of his life.

And at the last, as he looked out at the world through dying eyes, he realised that there was no beauty in death.

❄ ❄ ❄

How to Stay Afloat
When Drowning

Daniel Braum

*

Montauk, New York

I figured slipping away to the bar would be a good way to escape the table's cringe-inducing conversation, but I can still see Uncle Roy and Alison, laughing it up with the Client and our hired boat captain among the litter of cracked lobster shells and half-eaten fish platters.

The bartender sees me coming and is ready with another rum and coke. The night wind blows a gust of clean ocean air into the dock's aroma of fried food and cigarette smoke.

"Enough fishing talk for you, buddy?" the bartender says over the miasma of tables full of high-season out-of-towners here for something the fast-paced Hamptons can't offer.

He knocks on the wooden bar top and collects the dollar bills pinned under the tea light burning in a thick shot glass.

"I prefer my meals without talk of buckets of blood and guts," I say. "Thank you very much."

From over my shoulder a laugh joins the murmur of lapping waves audible in the second before the next classic rock song kicks in on the tinny speakers.

The bartender and I both turn to look at the woman on the stool next to me. She's in a long sun-dress and a green army surplus jacket despite June's warmth. There's no make-up on her young face, but she doesn't come across as young; the way her lithe frame is comfortably parked on the bar stool speaks of years. I think there's something unusual about her forehead but it's just the glow from the light strings hanging above the bar flashing on and off her face.

"What's so funny?" I ask.

She's staring past me at the water. I don't think she's going to answer.

"Everyone knows the real way to chum for sharks is to cut yourself from nape to navel and let your guts spill out," she says.

I expect her to laugh again, or at least smile. She doesn't.

The bartender winks at me and steps over to serve an old Italian man who has come up to the bar.

"We're uh, talking metaphorically here, right," I say. "Spill as in, spill into life? Your life, my life? Not into the water, right."

"Sure. Yeah sure," she says, blankly.

I feel like I've disappointed her and she's searching my face for a hint of the answer she wanted me to say. I know I should be uncomfortable with the way her gaze remains on me but I'm flush with excitement.

"Come on, you know what I mean," she says.

I *don't* know what she means but I smile like I do.

"I'm not really one for chumming," I say.

"But you're bleeding all over the place."

There's a splash from baitfish jumping below.

"You better look out... there may be sharks *about...,"* I half-sing.

It's her turn to smile at me with no idea of what I'm talking about.

"Sorry. My singing's terrible, I know," I say. "The real lyric is *dogs* not *sharks* though... never mind."

"I get it," she says. "Sharks smell blood like some people smell weakness."

At the table the Client and Uncle Roy are pretending they're holding rifles and aiming into the air.

I try to fight away the memory that comes. I'm surrounded by a mob that's pulling a six-foot thresher out of surfer-crowded waves and I'm squeezing Nina's hand.

"Fear isn't strength, it's just...thrashing," I mutter.

"Strength is in truth. The real kind of truth vulnerability brings," she says.

"Not too many people feel that way or would even comprehend that."

"You do," she says. "But you're here to hunt?"

I'm not here to hunt. There's no way I'm going out with Alison and them in the morning. There's no way to tell her without spiraling into everything I don't want to talk about. I almost say 'I'm just here to get through the day', but even that intentionally casual answer leads to unwanted paths.

"I'm only here for my family," I say.

She laughs again.

"What?"

"Tell me something true," she says.

"That is true. That's my sister sitting over there with my Uncle Roy. She runs the surf apparel distributorship our parents founded. The guy next to her is the purchaser for a big group of stores. So yeah, the point of the weekend is to land his business. The other guy is the boat captain my sister hired to take us out tomorrow. He told us his full name but he insists we call just him Captain Mike. He's a *bit* too serious about the Captain part of it too, if you ask me. Boring stuff."

"Then tell me something else."

"I don't know, like what?"

"Do you surf?"

"Never been on a board. Yeah and my family's business is surfing, go figure."

She swirls the ice in her glass, slides a few cubes through her lips then covers her mouth as she shifts her lower jaw. I think I hear a little pop.

"I… lived out here one summer," I say. "Feels like a lifetime ago. It was."

"What *was* it like?"

"Nothing like now, the town's grown up so much since—"

"No. What was it like for you?"

"Me? I was young, though I didn't feel young at the time. I felt alone and far from home. Then I fell in with someone. We were sort of engaged and… what can I say, we ran away together. That's what it was like."

"Almost sounds romantic," she says.

"I wish it was. It should have been. It wasn't."

"Are there really any good places left to run to?" she asks.

"We found a place in the middle of nowhere. Costa Rica. They have bats down there we wanted to see. This kind that grab fish right from the water. We had to take buses, and a little plane, and then a boat. The boat had to go... well the whole thing was a mess. Did you know whirlpools were a thing? I never knew they were real. And a thing to worry about when you navigate into the mouth of a river from the ocean. That's how I know. For a while there we thought our boat was going down. I'm not the praying type but I swore if we got out of it alive I'd never leave sight of land again."

"Wow, careful," she says.

"Don't worry. I'm not going out tomorrow. No way."

"I meant careful, keep being honest and vulnerable like that—"

"...and I don't know what I'll attract."

"I guess that too," she says. "I was going to say careful, you might get used to it."

We stare past the diners and drinkers at the crescent moon and the red dot beneath it. I wonder if she's going to speak. I like that she isn't about small talk, that she dives right into the heart of things.

"Can I get you another drink?" I say. "Better yet, I'm dying to get out of here. You up for a change of scenery?"

"It's late."

"Yeah, the days start so early around here. How about just one more?"

"It's not that," she says. "I'm here for my family too."

I want to ask *her* to tell *me* something true but it feels like the moment to ask that has passed.

"If I stay I'm going to have to go back to that table and talk about fishing and brand name wet suits," I say. "So I'm gonna walk these drinks off. If you're feeling like company and want to walk and talk with me, just say the word."

"I've already stayed too long. I have to find my sister."

She stands. I awkwardly wish her good night and mumble something about how I understand family comes first instead of asking her name and if I could see her tomorrow. She weaves through the tables and disappears into the door leading to the inside part of the restaurant and the parking lot and road beyond.

The bartender returns and shakes his hand like he's just touched an oven.

"Now that's a keeper if I've ever seen one," he says. "For a second there I thought you were going to reel her in."

I pay my tab and ask him where else is open around here this time of night.

"You could count the places on one hand," he says, then tells me.

I return to the table. Captain Mike and Uncle Roy are lighting cigars. Uncle Roy implores me to join them.

I politely decline, remain standing, and announce that I'm hitting the hay.

Alison whispers in my ear as I peck her cheek and wish her goodnight.

"You look pale. You okay?"

I nod and smile to let her know that I am.

"Goodnight," I say to the table. "See you all in the morning."

I don't mind lying to them though I'm kicking myself for not having the presence of mind to ask the woman for her name. I hope it's not too late to catch up.

Headlights from the road briefly light up the neighboring dock as I make my way through the tables. One of the busboys is standing on the shore having a smoke.

Somewhere in the dark a night bird calls.

The dock where I spent so much time with Nina isn't far from here. Salt air smells the same ten years on and isn't easily forgotten. I try to conjure the feel of her hand against mine. I'm not sure which memories are of real sensations and which are just fabrications dulled by the years. Wind rustling the sea grass brings the sense of vast open stretches of sand back to me. The night bird's honking cry echoes over the water...

The ocean breeze has tussled Nina's black bob into a wild tangle framing her sun-touched face. I can smell her last cigarette, though she swears she's quit. She leans in and rescues our melting ice cream cone with a well-timed lick followed by a big sloppy smile that transforms her. She ceases to be the depressed soul who thinks and talks so much about Art School but never paints. I no longer see the street-wise girl, running away from school, from the city, from what she calls 'conformity and everything' but instead she is an ethereal, sensual, carefree being, here watching the waves and afternoon surfers with me. Me. The would-be surfer who's never stepped on a board. With the afternoon sun warming my shoulders through my t-shirt and her sticky hand around mine I think maybe this is all life is, pairing up and running away from whatever it is you are running away from. Together. Like this.

The end of the pier is crowded with people fishing, holding hands, and wave-watching like us. The break isn't so hot but there are still surfers out there hoping the left will develop.

Someone in the water is yelling. Nina and I push over to the railing to look with everyone else. A young man has hooked a thresher shark on a line. The panicked fish spins and spasms as it is hoisted from the waves. A half-dozen people have their hands on the line helping bring it up. The shark swings and manages to smash itself into one of the concrete support pylons. The people pull and pull and bring it up all the way to the rail. A woman leans over and gets her arms around it. Someone holds her waist and pulls her in. The crowd grabs hold of the shark, lifts it over the rail, and drops it on the pier. It flops and twists, its open mouth revealing a maw of dangerous teeth and the steel hook that snared it protruding from its lower jaw. No one wants to go near it now. A widening circle of space forms around it as everyone backs up. The woman who first grabbed it emerges, brandishing a baseball bat. Her blow connects with the shark's side, right under its dorsal fin. It flips, landing on the steel hook, driving it deeper. The woman slams the suffocating thing again, then the mob is all over it. This isn't fishing. This isn't protecting anybody.

Our ice cream splats onto a puddle of blood and salt water. The shark is beaten into an unrecognizable shape. I realize Nina has never seen tears in my eyes. In the chaos of kicks and bat swings and skin and scales it dawns on me we're drowning. We're drowning here.

"Let's go," Nina says.

"I'm with you."

"No. I mean it. I mean let's really get out of here."

"Anywhere you want," I say. "Anywhere at all."

The silver setting reminds me of a wave curving around the small blue opal and two tiny diamond dots. The plan is to ask her to marry me at the lodge, at night, after we see our first fishing bat.

"Maybe I'll draw a bat while we're down here," Nina says, all the bouncing on the dreadful road making her voice vibrate funny.

The awful bus ride doesn't dampen her spirit and she kisses me as we lug our bag from the bus stop to the shore. The roaring ocean and clean air are so welcome. We're warned by the two boatmen not to go in while we're waiting for all the passengers. After ten minutes or so they decide there are no other passengers. There's water in the bottom of the wooden boat. The older man

148 of Daniel Braum

pushes off the beach and jumps in. The boatman on the motor guns it as we crash through the wave line. The boat catches air and lands with a heavy thunk. The older boatman leisurely bails water with a half of plastic jug.

We motor to the estuary at the mouth of the river which is the only way to the lodge. Swells lift and drop us. I don't like the look of the waves we're going to have to pass through nor the way the boatman are bickering in Spanish.

"It's rough," the younger boatman says to me. "We may have to go back and try again tomorrow."

"But it's almost dark," I say. "Where are we going to stay?"

"Don't sleep on the beach," he says. "The sand flies are not very nice."

The men speak to each other in Spanish.

"We're going to try?" I ask.

The boatman guns the engine. I grasp Nina's hand. The water in the bottom has soaked our packs. The older boatman is bailing in earnest now.

A big swell lifts and drops us. We spin and spin and wind up with our port side facing land. The boatmen men yell at each other as the boat is dragged along parallel to shore. Waves hit from all sides, the water fills up faster than the old boatman can bail.

"Can you swim?" the boatman asks.

"What's happening?" I ask.

"Kiss your wife and pray."

The older boatman stops bailing and throws a small wooden crate overboard. Then a full jug of something, motor fuel maybe. Then a bag of oranges he has fished out of the calf deep water. He grabs my pack and I stop him. We watch the jettisoned stuff spin away in the current. Large dark shapes are moving beneath the surface; I spot a lone dorsal fin heading toward the crate.

Nina is perfectly calm though she is squeezing my hand as hard as can be. Behind her a big wave is coming up on us sideways. Her look of resignation inspires a burst of sadness and anger. The boatman guns the engine. The wave slams us. We're soaked but somehow we don't go under and emerge from the blinding spray shooting towards the shore.

The sweet woman who runs the lodge escorts us to our cabin which is on a secluded rise nestled into tall palms at the edge of the rainforest. Through the big window taking up most of the far wall we can see the water that almost dragged us down. There is an assortment of pots and pans, a hair dryer, a small electric radio, towels, a flashlight and a can of bug spray lined up on the counter next to the sink in the kitchen area. A thick extension cord runs through the front window bringing power. The shower runs on rain water. We thank her and flop our bedraggled selves onto the big bed. When the woman leaves Nina cries softly. We fall asleep in our soggy clothes; the distant sound of waves no comfort.

We wake in the night. The waves have quieted. The tide has receded. A coral reef and fish are visible in the clear water, their tropical colors illuminated by the full moon. The balcony outside the window is bigger than my apartment. A metal tub, a coal grill, and bucket are the only things on it. We peel ourselves out of our clothes, heat up buckets of water, and fill the metal tub.

From our bath we watch the fish in the water below and spot bats flying by grabbing insects. I rub Nina's shoulders gently and whisper "we made it". This inspires a fresh round of sobs.

"What is it? What's wrong," I ask.

"People don't get it."

"Get what?"

"They don't understand the only thing that's real is how we treat each other. Nothing we do is going to be remembered."

Nothing I say comforts her.

After an hour I decide to trek down the cliff to the main area to see if I can find ice cream or anything that might cheer her up.

I return to the cabin and notice the big window is open and the power cord is running through to the balcony. Nina's stopped sobbing. I don't like the low-pitched buzz coming from outside.

"Nina?"

She's motionless in the tub. Her head's tilted back, staring at the sky with that same awful resignation that came over her on the boat. I'm confused at why the cord is out here until I see the submerged hair dryer. A blue arc jumps from Nina's bruised skin joining the pink and orange bolts that crackle over the water every second or two. The awful sound is coming from the radio floating by her feet. The reek of ozone and burnt hair hits me and I understand that what she has done was no accident.

I told myself a lot of nevers that night. Never leaving sight of land is the one I've kept. I must not have truly meant the rest. I spot the woman from the bar on the bend of the dark road up ahead. I walk faster to try and catch up.

The shape I thought was the woman is not a person at all but a big owl perched on road kill on the shoulder where the road turns onto Main Street just past where a bunch of cars are parked. The owl sees me, opens its wings and silently lifts into the air.

A man ambles out from behind the nearest car and crosses the road. There's something wrong about his face. He stumbles into the brush and beach scrub on the other side. I realize there's a path to the beach there and I follow him.

A dozen surfboards are half-buried in the sand forming a circle around a small bonfire. Dozens of people, surfers, are drinking and smoking and milling about in the fire-glow. The man stumbles towards them. In his path, I see the woman from the dock standing just outside the ring of light.

I run over.

152 | Daniel Braum

"Holy shit, you scared the hell out of me," the guy says.

The woman is nowhere to be seen. I spin around looking for her on the beach and in the crowd of surfers.

"Sorry. Uh, hey, did you see which way the woman who was standing right there went?"

"I didn't see anybody," he says.

His face is a patchwork of healed-over burns and scars.

I point to the sand. There's an indentation that's much too big for footprints. It looks like a person or two had been laying there.

"She was right there."

He shrugs and fishes a bright pack of cigarettes out of his pocket. He takes one out, lights it up and pulls deeply. I introduce myself and ask if I can bum one.

He hands me the pack and motions for me to take. Words on the wrapper say *Busa Buka Baki*. The cigarettes are cloves, wrapped in thin white paper. In what far-away place were these purchased? What a life he must have. They all must have.

I scan the beach looking for her again. I spot another of those big indentations in the sand a few yards away.

A tall surfer breaks away from the pack by the fire and comes over.

Every inch of his lean swimmer's build is sun tanned. His hair is bleach blond and he's wearing board shorts and a T shirt like the rest of the young people but the lines on his face show he is older than me.

"Everything alright?" he asks the scarred guy.

"Yeah, sorta, this guy scared me but everything's cool."

"This is a private party," the surfer says to me. "Do we know you?"

"No. And sorry, I didn't mean to crash. Or startle anyone. I'm just looking for my friend."

"You see her?" he asks.

"No. But maybe I can have a look around? To be sure."

A big splash at the shore carries through the darkness before he answers.

"Hey, Danny, I think someone's out there," someone by the fire calls.

The surfer and the scarred guy go to look. I palm the pack of smokes and slide them into my back pocket. I used to lift smokes the same way for Nina; even though I didn't want her to smoke, I knew she would and we couldn't afford it.

There's no one there, just the sets of waves coming in. People are leaving the fire-lit circle to check it out anyway. There's no thrill being here for me. I've come so far from the time I so desperately wanted to be a part of something like this. I return to the road and trek back to my hotel room.

Despite the hour, I cannot sleep. I wish I had told the woman at the bar that I didn't come to hunt; I came for Alison. I did think there'd be something here for me. That I'd be full of memories of Nina. The ache is so dull and far away it is almost not real.

I take a clove from the pack and smoke it. When it burns down I light another one. Nina thought stealing was wrong so I never told her where the smokes came from. I sit and smoke and imagine what it would be like to connect a swing of a bat into the sides of each of the surfers out on the beach. I know it's terrible but I don't care. Nina thought killing the shark was wrong. She'd probably think it was wrong to beat that mob who did it in. I never had the chance to tell her how I much I longed to do that.

I used to believe there would always be good places left to run to. Now I'm not so sure. Determining if there are any good places left to come back to seems more important.

Our warehouse was in Hauppauge, less than two hours away when the traffic's right. It was more like home than our house ever was...

There's a hint of saw dust and vanilla pipe smoke in the air, which means Dad's in his workroom shaping a board. Mom is gathering all signs of our domestic activity in the conference room the four of us have made our de-facto dining space and finding hiding places to obscure them from visiting eyes.

"Go get your father before you leave for class," Mom says. "The buyer should be here any second. Tell him it's the Professor, he'll know who."

The whine of the motor on Dad's wonky power sander grows louder as I walk through the rows and rows of stock, shelved wet suits and shoe boxes, towards the corner of our warehouse Dad has claimed for his personal workspace.

I push through the hanging plastic barrier into Dad's world. Remnants of past projects, experiments, and abandoned works in progress fill the small, square space; a test section of planed hardwood, a rack with two shaped but unvarnished boards, dozens of fins.

Dad's at the machine in the center of the room grinding a piece of wood that will one day be a surfboard. His long, dirty-blonde hair is tied back. Oversized safety goggles mask his clear blue eyes. He clenches his stubble-covered jaw in concentration.

The fins fascinate me the most. Dad could easily make standard designs. Easy sells to buyers but he makes all kinds of crazy boards with all sorts of fin positions.

"What kind is this one going to be," I say to announce my presence. "Single fin or double?"

One style is all the rage right now but I can't remember which.

"Neither. When it's done, I'll know."

"Mom says someone's here for you."

"A buyer? This late?"

"Mom said you'll know who."

This inspires Dad to stop the machine. He flips his goggles off.

"It's almost done, want to try it with me?"

"Now?"

"No better time."

"I dunno. I'm heading to class. I'll walk with you up front."

I know he's not pushing. He's trying to instill in me the notion to take on the world, on my own terms and at my own time. I grew up with him telling me you don't know if you can surf until you try and I love him all the more for it.

He shuts the lights and the power and together we walk through the rows of inventory towards the front. He's muttering to himself as we walk.

"When you are taken by the undertow, if you are lucky you realize you are but a river in this dark sea," I discern him saying.

"What's that?"

"Something for this meeting."

"What's it mean?"

"It's something surfers say."

"Come on, tell me."

"If I could I would."

Mom has transformed the conference room back into a showcase for our business. I grab my book-bag and leave Mom and Dad talking about waves.

As I'm getting into my car an old gray fiat with an empty surf board rack on top pulls up.

"Going to school, young man?" the man in the car, who I take to be the buyer, says through his rolled down window.

"Yes, sir."

"Good," he says. "All my best surfers do, I like that."

When Mom and Dad did not show for work the next morning Alison and I realized they were gone.

The police and the insurance investigators pointed out that the bank accounts were untouched and no valuables, personal items nor a single piece of inventory was missing. Except for whatever Dad was working on. His surfboards and parts and experiments were the only things unaccounted for.

Alison kept the business going fueled by the belief they'd be back. Later that summer, right around when Uncle Roy showed up to help her, I left. I'd only gone out East, but the East End might as well have been the ends of the earth when it came to the warehouse and my sister.

✳

Knocking on the door wakes me.

"Come on. Time to go," Alison is calling from outside.

I get up and crack the door. Morning light leaks in.

"I'm staying behind, sis," I say, pretending my best to sound ill.

"You okay?"

I open the door more so she can see my face, to let her know that I am. The door pushes inward; the security chain stretches taught preventing it from opening. It's Captain Mike.

"That's not how you treat family, son," he bellows. "Get your ass out here. Your client is waiting down at the dock."

Alison maneuvers him out of the way.

"It's okay, I got this," she says.

I'm about to say thank you when I realize she's talking to Captain Mike.

"Can I come in?" she asks.

I let her in. We sit on the edge of the bed. She takes my hand in hers and I know she is asking me to come on the boat.

"I'm not leaving sight of land," I offer as an explanation. "I promised myself after..."

"I know," she says. "It must be so hard for you to be back here."

"I'm fine," I say.

"The Client won't go without you," she says.

"Why the hell not?"

"How am I supposed to know, he just won't. Bad luck. Superstition. Misogyny? All of the above?"

"Tell him to fuck off."

"Believe me, I want to. The point of this weekend is to land his business though."

I realize how little I know of her. I know who she *was*. When we were a family. Before I left. From the few times we spoke I remember she'd broken someone's heart or had her heart broken, maybe both. Her life, as far as I know now, is keeping the business alive. And I don't think there's much else.

"Are you going to be okay if he doesn't sign with you?"

She shakes her head, no.

"Uncle Roy thinks I should give up, cash out, and sell the business."

"Why'd you even invite him to come?" I say.

"I wasn't sure you would."

We sit in silence.

"Where's the Client now?" I ask.

"On the boat, with Uncle Roy, waiting for us."

I grab my clothes and take them into the bathroom to get dressed.

The sensation of being pulled sideways in waves comes over me while pulling my shirt over my head. I stumble into the shower curtain.

"You okay in there?"

"Yeah, I'm okay. I'm coming. Just give me fifteen minutes to get coffee."

"Maybe you're not a pussy after all," Captain Mike grumbles under his breath as I leave the room.

"Does your boat hold water?" I ask in reply.

"What the fuck kind of a question is that," he says to Alison. "Where's he going?"

"To get coffee," she says.

I head for the diner Nina and I used to go to on Main Street, next to Lisa's bait shop. Most of the fishing boats are already out. There's no break and the waves are free of surfers. I turn onto the street and join the early-riser tourists walking leisurely from storefront to storefront. The only vehicle traffic is the knife-grinder truck crawling along, announcing its presence with a song on its old-fashioned bells. The truck gives a gentle honk as it passes the hardware store, which I'm amazed is still open for business. I see old Harvey Levitin behind the wheel and give him a wave. He returns the wave without any expression of recognition. A young mail guy is delivering to businesses that have sprung up since I was last here.

The diner next to Lisa's has been replaced by a frozen

yogurt shop. It doesn't sell coffee. I wonder how long it will take me to find some and make it to the dock. I look to see if a new place has opened up and see the woman from last night walking my way.

"Hello," I call.

She doesn't respond. I walk over and match her pace.

"Hello. Good morning," I say. "I'm so glad I ran into you. I went looking for you last night. Right after you left. I didn't ask your—"

Her mouth opens into a smile revealing a maw of jagged, triangular teeth. They are sharp and pointed and much too big. The edge of each tooth is serrated with small barbed notches.

I stop and squint, her face now showing no sign of the sharp-toothed monstrosity. She continues walking. I watch her pass the bait shop then double back and go around the side. She's not the woman from last night. Her hair is slightly shorter and she holds herself differently, otherwise she looks exactly like her.

An ambulance turns on to the road and speeds towards us; lights on, siren silent. It gives a brief chirp; the tourists move the minimum distance to give it space. The mailman crosses the street to my side after it passes. I walk to him and ask, "What was that all about?"

"Someone was killed," he says.

"What? Here?"

"Late last night. Beach's full of cops."

"What happened?"

"Who knows? We'll know when they tell us, right?"

We watch it turn left towards the beaches and docks and the path I came upon last night. I want to follow the ambulance. I want to follow the woman. There is no time for either.

＊

The Captain's forty foot convertible, the Lady Luck, is the only fishing boat remaining at the dock. An American flag attached to one of the antennae on its cabin tower flaps in the breeze. Alison, Uncle Roy, and the Client are on deck watching me approach. I can see Captain Mike inside the open cabin fiddling with the gear and switches on the console.

I step off the dock onto the boat's weathered rail, then onto the cushion of one of the built-in seat benches, then the deck.

"Hey, coffee boy," the Client says. "What happened, no coffee?"

His playfulness is grating. He's so chipper I wonder if he's still drunk. Uncle Roy puffs on a cigar, watching for my response. Is he wanting everything to fail?

"Who needs coffee when we've got eels," Captain Mike says saving me from having to speak. He exits the cabin hauling a white five-gallon bucket in each hand.

"Ready to land some Stripers? Don't let anyone tell you they like squid. This is my 41st summer doing this and I know the bass love this eel."

The edge is absent from the Captain's voice when he directs us to help by untying the ropes holding the boat to the dock. I think he might actually be trying to be pleasant.

"Hold onto your hats," he says. "It's a fine day for fishing."

I hope it is. The Lady Luck leaves the inlet and speeds into the Atlantic.

❊

I'm not happy when the last glimpse of Long Island disappears from view.

The steel gray ocean water is mercifully calm. The sky is clear. The sun is warm. I imagine it is a fine day for fishing. Captain Mike has classic rock playing on the radio. We can hear him singing along over the sound of the engines and gulls hitching a ride in our aerial wake.

He spots something on the fish finder and stops the boat.

He secures our rods in metal holders attached to the rail and helps us bait them. We're told we're over a school of striped bass. Within minutes I watch Alison land the first fish, then every few minutes someone is pulling a two or three-footer from the water.

Captain Mike brings two coolers from the cabin to the deck. One is for storing the fish. The other is full of iced beers. Uncle Roy and the Client each crack open a can. Alison waves her hand-held video recorder in front of them asking them what they've caught. They raise their beers proudly and hand one to me and the Captain.

Captain Mike declines because he is driving the boat and "on duty". I make a show of drinking one with them though a hundred beers aren't going to help me feel any better.

Captain Mike steps in front of the camera.

"I was driving the boat that pulled the world record 70

pounder out of the Sound. There are seventy pounders out there. Who wants a world record?"

We boat farther and farther out following schools on the boat's fish-finding sonar. The Client tells us stories of how his family brought him fishing when he was young and he doesn't seem like that much of a dick. Uncle Roy joins in by telling stories of how much Mom and Dad loved to surf and fish and finally pulls his weight by working in how they were such geniuses in business.

After we fish the next school Captain Mike adds heavier rods and reinforced line into the holders.

"Ready for more or ready for lunch?" he asks.

"We're drinking our lunch," the Client says.

They are such children.

"I suggest you put some grub in your stomach as there's no yakking on Lady Luck," Captain Mike says.

He breaks out the sandwiches he has packed. We sit on the deck benches eating his deli meat sandwiches wrapped in wax paper and foil and throwing bait to the gulls who grab it in the air. The boat rocks in the gentle swell. Alison seems carefree. For a second I almost forget how unhappy I am to be here.

Something strong is pulling on the Client's line. His rod has bent into a shepherd hook.

Captain Mike scrambles from the cabin.

"Pull 'er in, pull 'er in," he gloats.

"I'm trying," the Client says.

His reel is spinning.

"Okay, give it some, give it some. Let her take it. Wait for her to stop."

About half of the line goes out.

"Now crank," Captain Mike barks. "Want me to take a turn?"

Captain Mike and Uncle Roy and the Client take turns giving line and pulling in.

The client insists Alison take a turn. She passes me the camera. I get a shot of Uncle Roy against the rail trying to spot the fish.

About fifty yards out something jumps from the two-foot waves. A shark. The unmistakable dorsal remains above water for an instant before disappearing.

Captain Mike yells a mix of "hell yeahs" and indiscernible hoots before he switches to English.

"That's a ten-footer, out there," he hollers. "At least."

He instructs the client to take over the rod and reel from Alison.

"You want this fish?" he says to the Client.

"Yes," the Client says.

"Then dig in, this is going to take a while."

"You want this fish?" he asks to Alison and Uncle Roy in turn.

"Then put down that camera and get ready to fight," he yells. "Now we're fishing."

The damn guy is actually trying to give Alison her money's worth.

The Client yells a pathetic imitation of Captain Roy's hooting.

"Now we're fishing," I whisper.

They've wrangled the tired shark up against the side of the boat. Each section of rail is five feet long so we know the fish is over ten feet.

The shark is sleek and streamlined. The silver skin of its pointy head has a blue sheen from the sun and sky.

"Keep your hands away from its mouth," Captain Mike says.

He produces two sticks that look like broom handles tipped with a sharp metal barb. He drives one hook into the side of the shark and instructs the client to hold it. He sinks the other in the fish a few feet away and puts Uncle Roy on it.

"Hold it there. Just a few more seconds."

He lifts the cushioned top of one of the built-in seats and retrieves a short-barrelled shotgun.

The shark slaps its tail sending up a spray of ocean water. I taste the salt on my lips.

He pushes the barrel down, drops in two slugs, and pumps barrel back, chambering the first shot. Then he places the gun about a foot behind the shark's black eye and tries to hold it steady. The gulls on the tower take to the air in a noisy cloud when he fires.

My shoes are soaked with blood. All of our shoes are stained dark red. If Nina could see me now I would tell her I would do anything for Alison just like I tried to do anything for her.

When we reach the mouth of the inlet we can see the small crowd of people from the newspaper and fishing rags waiting at the dock. A crew of two men and a crane-necked hoist help Captain Mike get the Mako from the side of the boat onto the measuring gallows. It is almost twelve feet. The people from the papers are taking photos of the Client and Captain Mike with the shark hanging behind them.

I'd kiss the ground, for real, if everyone wasn't around. The Client is on cloud nine and thanks Alison for it, so at least I didn't break my word for nothing. The guy operating the hoist gives me the business card of his brother who is a butcher and the card of a friend who is a taxidermist. The small town doesn't feel as small as it used to.

A police car pulls up in the lot. Two officers get out and walk directly to us. They ask if they can speak with Captain Mike in private and escort him away from the hubbub to the soda vending machine under the extended roof of the shack that houses the restrooms. I watch the excitement of the day vanish from his face as they speak. Then he doubles over and drops to his knees. The officers help him up. One of them tries to embrace him. He pushes the man away and tries to hide his tears as he runs to his truck.

The surfer killed last night was Captain Mike's son. Someone opened him up the middle from neck to navel. The area on the beach where they found him is still an active crime scene. The Client insists on taking us to the bar and grill on the dock again to celebrate the catch anyway.

The place is less crowded than last night. A thing like a death is not going to stop people, mostly out of towners like us, from eating and drinking on a weekend summer night. Uncle Roy and the Client are drinking and smoking and holding court at the table for the seemingly endless amount of people who want to congratulate them on their catch over lobster and shrimp cocktails. The Client is flanked by two women he brought to dinner. He says they are his cousin and her friend on summer vacation but they are obviously two escorts from the city. Uncle Roy is in hog heaven. The bartender has named a cocktail for the occasion; he told me he did it under orders of his boss. Alison's downed several of his Mako Madnesses and I don't blame her because she's the one who is really stuck in the shit show.

I escape to the bar, again, to fetch another cocktail for her.

"Too bad it isn't September," the bartender says. "That fish would have won the shark derby for sure."

"How many sharks do they land in the derby?"

"I dunno. A lot. Real shame about Mike's son. I'm not fond of his Dad but Danny was a good guy. I hate what his stupid beach parties do for business but when he's here he always tips proper. Way back when he taught my kid to surf."

"Was he tall and blonde?"

"Like every other surfer, right? No surprise to anyone he was 41 and never settled down. Speaking of which, whatever happened with that young lady from last night?"

"Oh, I never caught up with her."

"That's a shame."

The Client and Uncle Roy get up from the table, receive a few last back-claps and handshakes, and then depart with the two women. Alison joins me at the bar and lets out the biggest sigh.

"He's going to sign," she says. "Thank you."

"I'm going to celebrate with a clove," I say.

"Cloves. Where'd you get them?" she asks.

"All the surfers smoke them," I say.

"I'll join you."

We go over to the busboy who's taking a smoke break on the beach where the neighboring dock begins.

"Off the record, Captain Mike is a dick," the busboy says as we smoke. "Harsh to hear about his son, though. There's a memorial bonfire going on tonight."

"Want to walk?" I ask Alison.

"Sure," she says. "I'm going to need a week to decompress from this."

We head away from the restaurant lights into the dark. Alison takes off her shoes and walks in the wet sand.

"Thanks for today," she says.

"I'm glad it worked out."

"He's happy as can be. This trip might become an annual thing, but I'll take that as it comes. You okay? You've been thinking about Nina all weekend?"

"Strangely no, something else. Something Dad once said to me."

She doesn't ask what. I don't blame her. It's been a hell of a long day.

"Need any help back at the warehouse?"

"Sure," she says without hesitation. "I'll need the help more than ever now."

"I've been thinking about sticking around. Count me in for Monday morning then."

I don't ask if she ever feels like she is sinking. She's too busy moving and keeping everything going to contemplate such a question.

"You ever wonder why Dad's stuff was the only stuff that went missing?" I ask.

I spot the bonfire up ahead. Even more people than last night are silhouetted in the glow.

"I still have Mom and Dad's boards," she says. "Their personal ones, from the house."

The smell of smoke and sound of rock and roll reach me together.

Someone between us and the fire is walking our way in the wet sand. We step away from the shore to allow her to pass by us easy. She changes course to keep right toward us. A woman. I recognize the elegant contour of her face. Is it the woman from last night? Or this morning?

The woman's lower jaw drops. In the dim light I discern those horrible teeth much too big for her mouth. Her arms do not end in hands but tapered triangles.

I push Alison towards the road. "Go," I say. "She's coming for me."

"What the fuck?"

"Go."

She sees my fear and takes a few steps.

The woman veers for Alison. I try to get between them and I trip on uneven sand.

The woman continues for Alison with only a glance at me. Her skin is rough and grey and full of texture. Someone emerges from the darkness. For a second I think I am seeing double and that there are two of the same person standing before me.

The first woman tries to side step around the second, but the second woman matches her step. She pushes Alison's attacker preventing her from getting around her. She is the woman I met last night.

"Go, get out of here," the woman from last night says to me. "This is my sister."

Her sister lunges for me. All I see are teeth.

The two sisters step side to side, their grappling an almost elegant dance. Alison reaches the end of the beach and disappears into the sea grass and dunes.

"I want her meat," the sister says. "Let me—"

"No," the woman from last night says. "Blood from sea for blood from land is not what we do."

The sister tucks her head and throws herself at her sister.

The woman from last night darts aside and her sister thuds down on the spot where she had been standing a second ago. She reaches for her sister's legs. Her thrashing throws up sand and shells and a spray of liquid that I hope is water.

I'm not certain of what I'm seeing; they are two women

fighting but their shapes are not right, something more than the almost darkness. I am sure the woman from last night is easily evading her sister's wild swings and thrusts, and that she's speaking, almost singing as she does. With each heave and thrust and bite the two of them wind up closer to the sea. When they reach the wet sand the fighting has stopped. The singing has stopped and I'm watching the two women walking into the water side by side. The receding tide pulls one of them out, leaving the other standing there, watching. I run to her.

"You saved me," I say.

I reach my hand around her back and pull her to me to kiss her. She pushes me away with one hand. The force causes me to stagger backwards and fall. She retreats from the water and stands over me looking down with only disdain on her beautiful face.

"I'm not here for you. I told you I'm here for her," she says. "To stop her from making a mistake."

Her face is the most beautiful I have ever seen. Her sleek, pointed head. Round black eyes. Silver skin with that hint of deep sea blue.

"I understand now."

"What do you think you know?" she says.

"Everything. Life. The currents. Tides. You showed me—"

"I showed you nothing," she says. "There is only one thing I want you to know..."

She takes my hand to her face and places my right index finger just inside her thin lips. A quarter inch slit opens in my skin where I touch her human incisor.

"...always remember the sharpness of our teeth."

172 | Daniel Braum

Something jumps from the water at the wave line. A fish. A shark? The shape is larger than I have ever seen in the shallows.

She moves her face close to mine. A raised notch pushes through the skin between her eyes. I try to look away. A single spiny antenna unfurls from the center of her forehead.

The spine ends in a pleasing shape, a fascinating shape, the shape of something to eat, a source of soft, gentle light in the darkness I cannot look away from.

I see water and waves; there are surfboards in the waves.

V-shaped gills open in a long, elegant neck. The mob carries a shapeless bloody carcass from the pier to the beach. Nina's face, happy and unblemished, dissolves into soft, yellow light, then all fades to darkness.

I wake up on the beach in the middle of the night. Sometime later, Alison finds me and helps me back to my hotel. I'm overcome with an aching emptiness, I don't know what from. There is only the terrible yearning, so terrible, but I don't know what for.

Monday morning, I show up at the warehouse as I promised. I get myself an apartment out East. On weekends I return to the town and watch waves like Nina and I used to.

❋

The night wind blows a gust of clean ocean air into the dock's aroma of fried food, cigarette smoke, and miasma of tables full of people. The glow from the light strings hanging above the bar flashes on and off the face of the young woman sitting next to me.

"Here for the shark derby?" I ask.

"Yeah my husband's going to get a record breaking Mako this time."

"How?"

"I just know it."

Her husband sees us talking and comes over from a nearby table.

"I was just telling him you're going to win the shark derby, honey."

"You a fisherman," he asks.

"Kind of," I say. "I try. What's your secret?"

"You can't ask that," his wife says. "A magician never tells his secrets. He's got the right lures though, I know that for sure."

She plants a kiss on him and runs her hands along his back.

"It's all in the chum," he says.

"Everyone knows the real way to chum for sharks is to cut yourself from nape to navel and let your guts spill out," I say.

They look at me like they expect me to laugh, or at least smile. I don't.

❋ ❋ ❋

GEODE

Rosanne Rabinowitz

*

Years ago, when I was 16, I disappeared.

Then I was found. Or more accurately, I reappeared, walking home out of the woods. I didn't show the effects of severe exposure though I was dirty and a lot thinner than when I left.

I didn't remember where I'd been. I still don't. But now I look out at the landscape of my childhood, hoping to hit that memory spot at last. I see a vast lake fringed by pines, rock-strewn shores and an occasional snow-covered beach that merges with the frozen snow-scattered water.

But I'm looking at the familiar shore through unfamiliar floor-to-ceiling windows in a large light room, so unlike the place where I once lived with my parents and my brother. That house was small and stuffy. It was hard to draw a breath without an accusation of snatching someone else's air.

When I was young, I looked out over the ice from my bedroom window and dreamed about the other side of the lake. When the frost drew patterns on the windows I imagined a formula that showed the way to another shore.

And behind the patterns on the glass, the fern and feather forests, I saw movement and the faces of folk. They were also clear-coloured like glass, shaded with a pearl finish by the frost. Sometimes they winked. Sometimes they leered but I wasn't scared. I regarded them as friends because I had no others, and wondered what they saw when they looked at me.

I tilt open one of windows because I hear something. First, it's only the muffled fall of snow from the window. Cold air comes snaking in but I don't close the window. There is something... a tinkling like glass chimes. The barest hint of bells or perhaps an old string instrument. A music box just for me. A stirring of the air that could be a voice.

Unknown, but almost familiar, hinting at lost time I came here to find.

Then I hear another voice...

"Nikki, I think they're in! The window's open and the lights are on. Hurry, get the pie!"

I close the window fast, as if caught in a shameful act. Indeed, where I come from – which is here – this would be considered a mad waste of heat.

The inevitable clamour at the door sounds through the house.

I should be pleased for a visit from these neighbours. In the old days in the old house, our next-door neighbours were a grim old couple who complained about anything that moved, especially if it was me or my brother.

This neighbour, who introduced herself as Anthea when our paths crossed a week ago, is a stocky pink-parka'd woman with a round smiling face.

I answer the door because after all, I'd rumbled myself by opening that damn window.

"Hiya neighbour... sorry I forgot your name. I'm awful with names. Nikki's gone to get the pie, she'll be over in a mo."

Her voice is loud and flat, the local accent. It makes me flinch because I once spoke like that. When I went to college I unlearned it with careful listening and repeating and watching myself.

I offer to make coffee.

Nikki will bring a pie, says Anthea.

Soon there's another knock on the door and I'm greeting a tall woman holding a foil-covered pie. Its fragrance reaches me from the open door. "Sour cherry," says Nikki. "With a layer of dark chocolate and dark chocolate shavings on top".

"What can I say but... come in?" I try to be jocular. In my short time away I'm already out of practice with socialising.

"This is my girlfriend, Nikki. *Nikki*, will ya cut that goddam pie?"

I try to hide my shock by offering Nikki the right knife for the job. She waves it in her partner's direction in smiling mock aggression before doing the business.

Anthea doesn't miss a thing though. "You seem surprised that we're gay. I bet you thought I was a dumb redneck more likely to tar and feather a lesbo than be a practising one myself. Admit it!"

She had me there.

"It's because I'm from this area myself," I tell them. "The boys would've been out with the torches for two lovely ladies like yourselves."

I should know, having been harassed for being a bit odd while I was growing up.

"You grew up here? What was it like?"

"I didn't enjoy it. I left as soon as I could. I live in Boston now."

I begin a flurry of noisy coffee-making to avoid saying more on that score. Conversations like this take a lot of effort, having to think about what I want to say about my life story.

"I've not come far myself," says Anthea. "About an hour south, a nothing town. Probably the same small-town boredom you had here, minus the lake and the scenery."

I nod. "Yeah, we have some top scenery here."

Yes, at least I had my little hidey-holes. And I need to visit the most important one. I feel anxious at the thought as if it will stir something up. But isn't that the idea?

"Beautiful place," says Nikki, looking about the lofty structure that I'm occupying. "We wondered when they were building it. More modern than the rest of the houses here... We only saw people around in the summer so we were pleased to see someone else move in."

"I'm just here until they get their summer people in. My parents used to live here. The new owners had this built after they sold the house and the land. And when I found out they were letting it out short-term I thought...

why not? I have a few things to sort out here and some time between jobs."

I'm glad no one asks me what I need to sort out. I offer to show my guests around.

Given that much of the house is open-plan it's a very short tour. The bedroom upstairs, the bathroom with its whirlpool bath. The basement with the CHP boiler chugging away on its diet of woodchips, and I mention the wind turbine turning on the hill behind the house. If you get a lot of anything around here, it's wind.

Then we have our pie and coffee.

Later I get on the computer and look at Facebook. There's a message from Cathy, along with a meme. I start to laugh. It shows a silver knuckleduster studded with big, extremely pointy quartz crystals. Written under it: "I'm gonna realign your chakras whether you like it or not!"

If only I had one of those when I was a kid. I touch a much smaller piece of crystal that hangs from a pendant around my neck. A fragment saved from long ago, though I had it mounted only recently. A reminder.

I suddenly miss Cath and set up a Skype call.

I thank her for the crystal knuckleduster.

"It's only a photo with a silly joke. It's not the real thing."

"That doesn't matter. It made me laugh. I love the idea."

Then I tell her about meeting the neighbours.

"I'd just assumed they were the sort of people I

wanted to get away from. But they turned out to be dykes. It's changed since I've been here."

"Did you tell them that that you're a *hasbian* yourself?"

I chuckle. "I haven't heard that expression in years, not since we broke up."

I talk about my plans for the next few days... looking at old articles from the local newspaper that haven't been digitised, visiting my old school and checking out any records there. Just walking around. Finding things out, uncovering the fragments that belong with the crystal that hangs around my neck. That seems important, though I'm not sure why.

Then Cath sighs. "I understand why you want to recover those missing days and how you get to a point where something like that gets important again. Just don't lose too many days of your current life."

"No way!"

We talk some more. More awfulness in the news and bands that are playing in Boston. Gossip. I start missing other friends. For I have nothing here besides a past.

My parents have been dead for several years. My brother, who I used to hate, lives in Australia. Once the last funeral and various money matters were settled we rarely communicate. For what would we say? He is a stranger to me, and I to him.

I try again to persuade Cath to visit. "It's a tourist destination, believe it or not! There's a beautiful lake, woods and what-not. People come from all over to visit the place I fought to get away from. It's funny..."

And I start laughing and can't stop for a while. I touch the crystal around my neck again and that calms me down.

✳

Later, I stretch out on my bed trying to sleep. I keep the blinds up in the window that faces me in bed. The same view of the lake and the woods I was looking at earlier today, lit by an almost-full moon and stippled by shadow.

I think of the patterns that intrigued me so long ago, patterns on the windows that hinted at leaves and mazes, ferns and forests. The shapes of snowflakes transforming to feathers and spiders, wings and whorls. Double-glazing and better ventilation put an end to those designs. Yet they've left a residue, which is etched in my mind if not the glass.

The people. Those folks peering out from under the ferns and between the trees.

I try to see them again and remember what they meant for me.

Angular faces and bodies made of angles, crystalline figures whose voices tinkled and shattered and reformed in showers of light. They are clear but not lacking colour, tinted with frosting.

As I feel myself drifting off, I make my nightly appeal to the place where memories lurk. The sub-conscious, the surly gate-keeper that keeps my own secrets from me.

Show me, asshole. I'm ready for it. You *bastard*.

Again, I probe that gap in my mind. It's like flicking my tongue over the spot where a tooth had been.

Over the years, I tried to find clues in dreams, especially those that come again and again. There's the one where a thick string is coming out of my mouth. I pull on it. It doesn't hurt. But it's wrenching and uncomfortable. I know that I'll feel much better once I get this thing out, and yes... the piece of string in my hand is getting longer, almost arm's length. Something's coming loose as I pull. I always wake up.

Then one time I actually pulled the length of string out and rolled it into a ball. That ball became a head. I tried to look at the head but couldn't bring myself to do it. I woke up.

Progress, my therapist said when I told her about that dream. That shows progress. We're getting there.

That was over five years ago.

We never got there.

But now I'm here.

Here where it all began.

As I drift off I demand again: What are you going to show me? Come on, I'm ready!

I didn't have time to think about that stuff the last time I was here. There was my dad's funeral – not long after my mom's. Since the house had already been sold we both stayed in town at hotels. We didn't even come to the lake shore or any of our old haunts.

As I drive into town I check out the changes. Last time, there was no organic café or bars selling microbrewery beer. Under other circumstances I'd be tempted by the coffee stout.

I go to the school first. I'd had ideas of walking about the building but I change my mind. Last thing I need is an altercation with the security guys. We had none of that when I went there, but things are different now. And fair enough. I wouldn't want a bunch of sentimental old fools wandering around any more than a shooter or a pervert.

But it's not schmaltz rising in my throat but something much more corrosive. The stink of the school corridor has hardly changed. The sweat-scent of anxiety mixed with antiseptic wash, swished over the floors by some glum-faced and no doubt underpaid janitor.

Despite the primary colour scheme and the CCTV cameras poised in each corridor it feels oppressively the same. On my way to the office I pass familiar places. There's the science room where I went regularly to pester my favourite teacher. One of the few things I joined in my school years was a math and science club. We hung out in the science room and helped with cleaning beakers, polishing rocks, that kind of thing.

We had an assignment to find an interesting rock. I brought mine in with an apology because it wasn't very pretty and didn't look like much at all, but its rounded shape caught my eye.

Ms Harris, that's the science teacher's name. No, *Miss* Harris. Back then, in this town, you were either Miss or Mrs.

Miss Harris was pleased with my rock though, and beamed when she picked up the rock and shook it. "Listen," she said. And I listened. "It looks like a *geode*. They're not common around here but you found one."

That marked a turning point of sorts. I started to concentrate on getting good grades and a scholarship. I went to school and carried on with the math club. Sometimes I appeared normal. I even dated a boy from the math club who was just as socially impaired as me.

But other times...

I would wake up in the early hours. I would hear my brother snoring in his room. Even and benign, the sound meant he wasn't alert enough to torment me.

Then I saw *them* just outside the window. Faces crowding together, translucent eyes wide. I heard the tinkling and clatter that could have been their language, or just the sound they make when they move.

Once they surrounded my bed, their fingers of ice touching me with curiosity. I laughed at them. If I met them for the first time now I might be frightened, but I had no fear then. The ice of their fingers made me shiver but it didn't last long because it melted on contact.

The next morning I was accused of wetting the bed. But the wet didn't smell. I knew it wasn't that. But no one believed me.

Stories like that get around, especially with a brother like mine.

I haven't thought about my brother much since our father died. The funeral and then the will was sorted out peacefully and then we went our separate ways.

But with the scent of school, the fumes of *eau de shit* education, I remember other things. I never *forgot* about them but it was always a blur, a mush of unpleasant experience.

It takes just a glimpse out the window at the end of the corridor as I knock on the office door. There's the tree I used to sit under with a book during lunch when the weather was good. It's not that kind of weather now but I remember what it was like in May.

My brother approaches with his gang of older boys. I hear his hooting crescendo of my name, the other boys joining in. They surround me... Lisa wets the bed. Lisa's lousy. Who wants to lay Lisa?

I guess they just go away and I go to my next class. I know I never had any solitary picnics under that tree again. I took my lunch to the science room instead.

No big deal. I'm sure others have seen much worse. He didn't thump me *then*. And even when he did... I'm here, I survived. More than that... I've done well with my math and science. Yay, Miss Harris.

They're polite in the office. I don't recognise anyone. Good, no one will recognise me. I ask about my records from 30-odd years ago and I'm met with a blank look. Those records weren't even put on computer. They might've been shipped off to an archive.

The bored young woman – well, I'd be bored too – gives me some email addresses and contact numbers to try.

I'm just about to leave when I remember another question.

"Do you have any contact information for a Miss... I mean Ms Harris still teach here? She taught science when I attended. I can leave my email address if you do."

An older woman at a computer answers. "Harris? I remember her. She passed away about five years ago. Cancer, I believe."

I'm surprised at how hard it hits me. Like a 16-wheel rig had just jumped off the highway and gets me right *there*, in my chest.

☀

I'm off, running down the corridor. In my car, blinking back tears as I steer my way back 'home'.

How can this affect me more than the death of my own parents? She was a teacher. I had no idea what she did with her time outside of school. I didn't really know her.

When I pull in the drive I sit in the car and think for a while. I reach under my jacket and scarf and touch my crystal pendant. The single piece I kept with me, but the rest I hid where he would never find it.

I go inside to put on warmer clothes suitable for a walk along the lake. Before I change I check my emails and send some to chase up my records. I welcome a few moments of distraction.

☀

Now that I'm walking along the lake shore I'm remembering more. Not all of it is bad. I really did love that lake. Swimming in the summer, skating in the winter... in designated areas. We were all very careful about skating and fishing but someone did die every few years. People told me later that the police had dragged the lake after I went missing.

Someone at school lost a younger brother to the thin ice. I wondered what she would feel every time she looked over at the lake and how she could face living here. Of course, she had no choice. I had no choice about where I lived. I also wished that the lake had taken my brother instead of hers.

It's a deadly time of year now... the ass-end of winter, but not quite spring. Thaws and freezes in different places at different times. But I liked the way that the ice outlines branches and twigs, the quiet drip and the fierce winds that bring another freeze.

The white expanse of the frozen lake exerts a fascination that mere water doesn't match. Just to think that this *could* be walked, even as far as Canada. I used to sit in my hide-out and think about it. I might have forgotten many things but I'm sure I can still find the place, just the other side of that rocky projection and thick cluster of trees.

It's sheltered from the wind, the kind of cove that could've hosted smuggled goods or drugs. At the time, it was simply a stomping ground for an ill-tempered teenager.

As soon as I step behind the boulders I know where I am. A few things have changed here... More erosion, more rocks here, less of them there. But like the school it feels very much the same.

I kick snow away from a rock and sit down. I used to hide shit around here among the boulders. Shoplifted makeup at a certain age. At another age, a book in a sealed baggie, put in a metal box. Later I filled the metal box with pieces of rock and crystal.

Crystals. Long fractal fingers that reach from inside the earth to make the meanest of knuckledusters. More durable cousins to ice, crystals formed from the sky. None of that namby-pamby 'healing crystal' stuff. Crystals are hard. They cut. They should be respected. I wish I could've been as hard as that, and that I could have cut as sharply.

They were what remained of the geode, the rock with the open space inside and its secret heart that rattled when Ms Harris shook it. She showed me how to take it apart carefully with a hammer and chisel and how to clean it. This revealed banded colours and crystals like teeth within it. Another world. A geode.

Although I've forgotten many things, the location of that box emerges in my mind without any effort. Will it jog the other memories that went AWOL? No, that place is still blank. I catch my breath.

I know what I *liked* to think. The frost friends or freaks or fiends took me away. It was a story I told myself, even though I was sixteen and too old to believe in fairies and imaginary friends. But what the fuck happened? There's no explanation so they could have taken me. Somewhere. A place I wanted to be.

At least I made it as far as Boston. From a teenager who stole makeup I grew into someone else, someone able to see a structure of the universe in an object I held in my hand. I became someone overcome by beauty that had nothing to do with disguise.

I thought Miss Harris would want to keep the geode in her science room. But she urged me to take it home because I'd discovered it. I should have left it with her. But I was also thrilled to take those two halves back with me and keep them on my window sill.

Then my brother found it and took another hammer to it. Not the thoughtful hammering that uncovered this wonder, but one that smashed it into fragments. I wear one of them. And I hid the rest of the pieces to keep them safe.

I'm sure I can find that box. Yes... it's in that cavity between two boulders, with stones that I put in front of it. I have my thick gloves on. All I need to do is move some stones aside and there it is.

I open the box and find the shards inside. They're all sizes, the crystals translucent with hints of pink and purple and blue. I'm pleased to find them but I'm ready to cry again, remembering how something I loved and treasured had been shattered.

He broke more than pretty rocks.

He would get at me, over and over, jabbing at me. On the upper arm, in the stomach. Tripping me, making me fall. Then laughing at me for being clumsy and telling everyone who'd listen that I was a clumsy person who couldn't do a thing.

I turn the pieces of crystal over and over in my gloved hand. He fucking smashed it, the fucker. He's far away in Australia so he can't bother me anymore.

"I hate him. I really hate him." I'd say to Mom or Dad, touching the bruises on my arm, a pattern of blue, green and purple... yellow at the edges.

"No, you don't. You think that now, but you really love him. He's your brother. You don't really think that at all. Families love each other even if they have arguments."

Same as being told I fell because I was clumsy, not because I was pushed.

I pick pieces of the geode from the box and try to put them together, as I tried to do many times in the past. Some are smashed too small, other pieces are missing.

I watch my tears falling onto my gloves and my dark fleece-lined snow pants. I'm sure they are freezing. They fall with a whisper, a barely audible passage of air. And as soft as it is, I also hear an answering murmur carried by the wind outside my nook.

Then another voice joins in. A deep melodic voice winding through the whisper of frozen tears. I'm sure that voice is entirely human and it's coming closer. I can't hear the words in a song flung about by the wind, but I don't need to. It's some sort of blues, a song of loss. It's a desolate song but beautiful too. I feel better for hearing it.

I scramble to the entrance of the cove. As I peer from behind a boulder, I see Nikki making her way along the shore.

I'm wondering what gave her cause to sing such a heartbroken melody.

I lift a hand up to wave at my neighbour and watch the frozen tears fall from my glove. I see answering glints from the field of ice in front of me... a response, a stirring. I see many of these tears, shed by thousands, turned into ice.

Nikki doesn't see me wave, and I decide not to disturb her further. I gather my box of fragments to take home.

I arrange them on my window sill. I don't try to put

them together again but leave them as they are, exposed and spread, each piece clear against the lake and the pine trees on the other side of the glass.

We're getting there, said my shrink when I told her about the cord coming out of me that formed into a head. Maybe that round thing had been my geode all along. But why would I be afraid to look at it?

Later, I'm in bed. I stare across the lake in my window and listen to the wind pushing against the glass. My geode fragments catch the moonlight.

And then I'm somewhere else. Sleep? Dream? Maybe. I'm standing at the shore. The wind is blowing, making me wish I'd put my coat on over my pyjamas. Yet I only feel the chill in the air around me but not from within, as if my skin provided its own insulation.

Then I walk across the ice.

It doesn't take long to cross the lake though I know it should be miles. Perhaps I crossed a border but there are no guards ready to check the passport I don't have in my PJ pockets. I do have my phone though. I take it out and shine its flashlight and feel more comfortable with that spot of electric light in the night-bright expanse of the lake. And somehow, I'm skimming over it.

The land and water is filled with static... a rhythmic sound of breaking. But the ice beneath my feet is still solid and I reach a shoreline even rockier than the one I know. Past a strip of beach where cliffs rise, fringed by pines. A rounded surface draws my eye, a curve among the crags. When I come close I see an opening. A curious gleam from within, barely visible.

I squeeze through the gap. I have to rub my eyes to make sure I'm actually seeing this... drunken crystal pillars tilt from the floor, descend from the ceiling, project from the walls. Some are clear. Others are stained with clouded tints of amethyst and green.

Wind pushes into the chamber and the whispering starts. A susurration of crystal and creatures that illuminate and cut. My mind grabs for the words they utter but it doesn't find them.

I move among the pillars, finding support when I'm not sure of my footing. Sometimes it's hard to locate a place to step but I want to go in deeper. Then I discover a slot where I can sit, lean against a slab and gaze at the ceiling.

My light beam catches multitudes of sparks above me. Giant crystals jut downwards, shaded in pearl. They create another landscape, poised over me.

Then I see *them*, all around, moving within the interstices. Flickers from within the crystals and more frost creatures emerging. Frost friends, now solid. Angular faces and limbs, glittering pale eyes.

I once thought they were friends when I didn't have any. Now I'm not so sure.

I try to look at them directly. But they dodge definition, they refuse to stay in a form I can recognise. Angles and facets... as soon as I see one set they slip into another, or they open into other forms that are equally elusive... angles and planes that can't be contained in my brain.

It makes me dizzy and somewhat sick-feeling. I clutch my stomach, look down at my feet instead and breathe deep and think.

That's why I couldn't look at the 'head' in my dream... maybe it was mine all along.

Then I straighten up. I can understand the structure if I touch it. The ice things will not hurt me. If they wanted to, they would have done so long ago. I stand on my toes and reach...

Upon contact with my skin the surface of the hanging crystals softens and grows pliable. I'm startled but I touch it further to see where this leads.

It begins to melt and move under my fingertips. I'm seized with guilt as I see other surfaces transforming around me. What have I done? Have I ruined this place?

We all dissolve but we rise again.

I'm slipping on the surface but the partial melt lets me move about more easily. I'm out and running across the ice.

I had my phone with me so why didn't I take a photo?

That's my first thought when I realise I'm in my bed.

The dream stays with me as I pad down the stairs to make coffee.

I settle with my cuppa at the computer, curl my toes into the carpet, try to ground myself. But the computer's cheerful boot-up chime makes me jump. My ears still ring to the voices in the crystal cave, a massive geode I could step inside.

Outside the sun is shining, many points of light reflecting on the ice. Drip-drip just outside my window, sound of a thaw, yet I know it can be deceptive.

I'm surprised to see an email from the school records people. I had little hope anything would turn up. But they'd actually scanned in old handwritten records. Someone must've been in a good mood somewhere. I try not to get too excited.

The document is in black and white, contrast turned up to make it crisp and readable. But I can imagine the yellowing paper and cardboard boxes.

"That was quick," I say to my computer.

Of course, they don't tell me much more than I already know. I was readmitted to school. Notes in various hands talk about 're-entry' problems. "Avoids contact with others."

"Sure," I say. "Like, who'd want contact with you anyway?"

It must've been that psychologist they called in to talk to me. This forty-something guy who asked: "Do you ever think about boys and sex?"

"No," I'd lied.

Then there's another note under 'recommendations'. "Lisa should be encouraged to follow her own interests. She has excelled in math and has also shown an interest in geology. Perhaps she'd like to join the county club?"

Note from Jane Harris. Jane... Did I even know that her name was Jane?

Tell me I'm a special snowflake, teach. I smile. Give the kid a rock.

But it also makes me quiver to remember. Miss Harris – Jane – had always been kind but I never knew the extent of her interest and encouragement. Did the fuckers listen to her?

A tear falls on my finger. Better there than on the keyboard. I go to the window sill and let the next one fall on one of the cracked crystals. Time to open a window. Need air. Need to hear the outside as well as look at it. That drip-dripping. I always liked that sound. But I also know the dangers of spring. The thin ice, the floods.

Very faint, coming across the ice, I hear a sound like a train. It chugs in an off-beat rhythm that no train ever made. There are no trains around here.

I look through the fringe of pine trees and the vista of the frozen lake. A ruined ice hut, half fallen in.

Here it comes, louder. A noise like plates of glass or stone scraping across each other. Surfaces of crystal scraping, a musical tinkle of breaking glass.

I hear voices again in the crunch. Delicate like the breaking glass, they make me see falling star-shapes with the sharpest of points, ready to draw blood. I've heard them before. An echo, a movement at my window. Grinning faces around my bed.

A dog from a house down the shore starts barking. Late winter sun flickers through the swaying trees. Their lines move and reassemble with more clinking.

A cloud of white rises on the horizon, a train in the distance raising dust, an ice locomotive moving across the frozen plain.

The frost things, my old friends. They're coming closer. I don't see them yet but I hear them.

"Nikki!" Anthea is standing in front of her house, fists on hips, frowning.

The ice is singing now in a thousand voices. For so long they've been shapeless, just on the edge of comprehension.

But now words are forming. *You're back, you're back.*

Sorrow iced and paralysed, cracking and springing free.

We're coming. We're coming.

Who are you?

Hear the thunder. Ride our wave.

We are coming.

What do you want, I ask.

What you want. What you want.

This becomes a chant. I'm not sure what I want.

There are no answers. Only a whispering and tinkling, a cracking and creaking and a breaking, a million chandeliers falling to the ground and shattering in the flicker of the sun.

A wedge rises from the lake. A mass moving on long ice fingers, rolling over, crawling, shattering and reforming.

It's coming. I open my window wider so I can hear better.

The advancing ice-wedge is twice as high as me. It throws up snow and glints in with all the colours of last night's cave. Its ice fingers propel it forward. A tree disappears under its crest, a bush is consumed. It's crawling up the wall, piling up and up against the house where I am staying. A gape-mouthed fish dragged from the depths of the lake stares at me.

"Lisa!" Anthea is calling up to me. "It's going into your fucking house!" Not hers, which is set back further and out of reach of its edges.

The wind flows into my open window. I put on my coat and pull on my boots and raise my hands to the gale.

"Nikki! Nikki! It's pushing in!"

In response Nikki strides out. She walks up to the ice wave and puts her foot on it, testing its stability. Then she takes out her phone and starts filming, with a nod up at me.

"Nikki, what are you doing? Are you climbing up that thing? Get away from it!" Anthea shrieks. She seems terrified. I start to feel sorry for her. I've been full of fear. In the past.

The wall of ice advances. *Will you ride the wave of spring? All your sorrows crack upon the shore. Ride the wave and tame them.*

"Call the fire service. Call the cops!" Anthea shouts.

I have to laugh. Of course I won't call the cops on my friends, who smile with pointed crystal teeth from their refuge in the wall of ice.

The shatter of ice is now met by the shatter of glass downstairs.

I step out of the window and jump onto the wave.

My friends are there and we are moving forward. We hold hands and raise them and stand in hundreds abreast as our wave keeps breaking upon the shore, and breaks the building that was never and will never be a home.

It breaks, it breaks. And I climb on top of the flow and rise.

❋ ❋ ❋

House of Faces

Andrew David Barker

＊

I returned to the old house after three years, or maybe it was four. My neighbourhood kind of looked the same, except cars cluttered the roads and windows were smashed in and the grass was long and a few houses had burned down. The same as every other street in every other town and city I had passed through. There is a monotony to the end of the world.

The air was still, the sky clear: a deep and beautiful blue. It had been hot and was getting hotter. The height of summer. My neighbourhood once smelt of cut grass and barbeques and rang with the sound of kids playing and ice cream vans and music floating along the breeze. There were girls in light, willowy dresses and guys in shorts, washing cars, drinking cold beers, laughing too loudly; there were dogs barking and air conditioning and the sound of someone hammering; there were books to be read and movies to watch and children to love; there were jobs to work and traffic to get stuck in and bills to pay; there were politicians to hate and sex to have and people to laugh with and hands to hold and gentle rages at the injustice of it all. We were so stupid. *I* was so stupid. There was once a steady hum of life and I took it for granted.

I came to my house. I'd lived in it for ten years before the end of the world. I lived there with my wife and my son. He was twelve when the end came. I was forty-one, my wife thirty-nine. I think I'm now forty-five, but I'm not certain. The past three or four years have left blank spots in my memory.

My house looked smaller than I remembered. The driveway was cracked, the front lawn was wild; my door was hanging off its hinges. A few windows were broken, but not all. The plastic frames were no longer white and the tree my wife planted over a decade ago had fallen and lay across my driveway, brittle and ugly.

One remarkable thing struck me. The bins were still out.

I remembered that I'd brought them from round the back of the house, wheeled them down the driveway, and left them on the pavement ready for the bin-men to come and empty them the next day. Only, the next day never came. Not in the sense we were all expecting anyway. It had always been my job to do the bins. It was my weekly ritual. That night, after I'd put the bins out, I glanced at the stars overhead, waved to Bill over the road, then went back inside to watch some TV show with my wife. I forget the programme. We went to bed early and were so tired we didn't even kiss each other. It was just another night. That all seemed like a very long time ago, and yet, there were my bins, where I'd left them. I couldn't believe that after everything that'd happened, after the entire world had been chewed up and spat out, my bins would still be there, waiting to be emptied.

The black plastic was sun-scorched and warped and weeds had grown up around their base. There were two bins, one for general rubbish and one for recycling, to help save the planet (ha!). I went over to them and ran my fingers over the lid. I gripped the handle. The last time I had done so I'd had a wife and child and the world was still turning. Now here I was, years later, and everyone was gone; my wife, my son, my mother, my father, my friends, Bill from over the road, every last fucking person on the planet. Except me.

I opened the lid and reeled back from the stench. I lifted the bandana from around my neck and covered my mouth and nose, before I returned to the bin. The rubbish inside was a massed clump, an almost indistinguishable block of crap. I could make out part of a pizza box, the logo completely faded from existence, and a plastic milk bottle, some mash of colours that may have been a magazine and, most astonishing of all, a pair of tights. My wife's tights.

I stared at them for a long time, then I fished them out, cradling the tights in my hands. I thought of my wife's legs, how dark and long and soft they were. I was astonished to feel a stirring in my cock. I hadn't thought of sex in what felt like an age and now here was the once-familiar urge creeping through me again. It was a good feeling, a human feeling: base desire and a swirl of erotic images. I felt quite giddy, but the moment was short lived. A deeper wave of feeling overcame me. A feeling that was all too familiar now. The feeling of loss – a deep, wrenching, shuddering sadness that felt beyond thought and reason. Like a corkscrew to the heart, as Bob Dylan once wrote.

I scrunched the tights up into a ball and shoved them into my rucksack, then I turned to the house.

There was a face at the window.

I caught my breath. I felt the sun burning my neck. The face was motionless, just staring out of the bay window of my old front room. It was difficult to make out in such blazing light and deep sun-shadows, but it was a face made of old curtains and dirt on the glass. I walked up the drive, stepping on and leaping down from the old tree my wife once planted. The face lost some of its form as I viewed it from different angles on my approach. I readjusted my direction so that the framing of the dirt in the curtains kept the semblance of a face. And it was a nice face. A happy face. The first face I'd seen for at least three years.

I walked round the narrow path to the bay window and gave the face a nod. At this close proximity however, the illusion was lost, so I stepped back into the forest that was once my front lawn and then positioned myself so the dirt aligned with the gaps once more and the face reappeared. Like magic.

"Hello," I said.

The face didn't respond, only smiled.

"Lovely weather we're having. I heard on the forecast that there's a storm on the way. I suppose it couldn't last. Not with this humidity. I do love a good summer storm though, don't you?"

Nothing.

"A good thunder storm, that's what we need. That'll clear the air."

The face carried on smiling.

"I know," I said. "The first conversation I've had with someone for nearly half a decade and I talk about the weather. Typical Brit, eh?"

The face laughed.

"Well, I better get unpacked..."

I stopped and listened to what the face had to say.

"Oh, I think I'm going to stay awhile. We'll see."

The face said something else.

"Yes, it's good to be home. I've been gone too long. I tried the coast and a few other cities and even spent a bit of time up on the moors, but this is home. You know what they say... home is where the heart is."

I bite back a surge of tears and had to compose myself. The face didn't notice though, which I was relived about because I didn't want to embarrass him or make him feel uncomfortable. After all, we'd just met.

"You too," I said, after a while. "I'll get settled in and maybe we could have a good old chin-wag later. Whadda you say?"

The face smiled.

"Great stuff, see you later."

I went into my house.

❋

The house had been looted, but it wasn't as bad as some places I'd been in. My front door – which was hanging on by a solitary screw – opened straight into the hallway and staircase. A few pictures had been knocked from the walls and smashed and there was glass all over the carpet, and several stains: blood maybe, animal piss, who knows what. I stepped inside, glass crunching under foot. There was one picture still hanging. The one at the foot of the stairs. The family portrait: me, my wife, our son, and even our dog, taken at a photography studio when our son was four. Our beautiful boy.

I looked at us. We didn't seem real anymore, but then, I suppose, we weren't real anymore. None of us. My wife, my boy, the dog, and even me, all of us were now ghosts. Only, I was a living ghost, a shell that once housed a human. I'd thought about their faces every day and every night since I lost them, and sometimes it had been hard to keep their images alive. But looking at them again, I recalled every aspect of their features; the lines on my wife's forehead, her mouth, her eyes, so deep and green and alive, and my son, angelic, innocent, blonde, and golden with the light of goodness and love.

Looking at them I felt detached, like I wasn't really in my house, staring at my family as we were over a decade ago. I closed my eyes and tried to hear our ghosts, tried to hear my son getting ready for school and my wife and I talking in the kitchen and the dog barking and the TV on. Then I opened my eyes and my family looked back at me and all was silent.

I dropped my rucksack and walked through to the front room.

A few things had been upturned, but aside from that it was much the same as it had been when we fled on that night long ago. The TV was gone, which amused me. Even as the world was falling and people were being taken, someone thought it prudent to steal my television. Humans – never let the apocalypse get in the way of a good opportunity.

There were more pictures on the mantel, mostly of our boy – opening presents at Christmas, first day of school, riding a donkey on a grey English beach. There was my wife, the natural light picking out the auburn in her hair, and one of me and her on our wedding day, so impossibly long ago I questioned whether I really inhabited the same body as the man in the picture. I may only be in my mid-forties, but I felt, and still feel, hundreds of years old to have seen all the things I have seen, experienced all the lifetimes I have lived.

I sat on my sofa. Dust kicked up as my frame disturbed its slumber. I sat in my spot, nearest the door, and looked over to where my wife used to sit. We watched TV here, we talked here; once or twice, we made love here. I looked at the pictures on the mantelpiece again and couldn't shake how strange this all felt. It always felt strange to look upon a human face – I'd seen many pictures on my travels, pictures of strangers, and it was always odd. Odd to look upon human beings. It was odd to catch sight of my own face, in reflections, in mirrors, in water. I looked like an alien being now, my internal self at odds with the person who carried me.

Faces are strange things when there are no faces left. Yet, nothing so far had felt as strange and as devastatingly beautiful and as sorrowful as looking at the faces of my family again.

Now home, I wondered why I had been away so long.

I looked to the bay window and from my position, in my favourite place, the gaps in the curtains lined up with the dirt on the glass and revealed to me the face, from a different perspective.

"You again," I said.

The face smiled back at me.

"I remember a Christmas morning in this room. It's strange to think of Christmas when it's so hot, but that one is sharp in my mind. It snowed heavily and my boy was maybe, five, six, and it was the first white Christmas he'd ever seen. I saw it through his eyes and it made everything magical. I think he still believed in Father Christmas then and his excitement filled us with such joy..."

I fell silent for a moment. The face waited patiently.

"We were capable of magic. At times we were... real magic. A magic that transcended the ordinary and showed the beauty in everything. Because I now realise there was no such thing as ordinary, but it was hard for us to see. A lot of the time..."

I looked at the face and his smile looked sad.

That afternoon I moved from room to room and memories came soaring into my head. The pain was great, but there was a strange kind of comfort in the sorrow. The kitchen – the heart of a house – was almost overwhelming. Our calendar was still up. A calendar made up of twelve of our favourite family pictures from the previous year – the last full year of Homo-Sapiens. The calendar rested on October, the final month. It was a photo of my wife and boy kicking autumn leaves in our local park. They were both laughing, holding hands, hearts beating.

There was still milk in the fridge. It was solid. Our table and chairs were there. There were plates on the drainer. I threw up in the sink and then moved into the back room.

This was used as a play room for my boy, and for me, I guess. Here was my old record player, one I'd had since boyhood, and there was a cabinet full of records. I sat on the floor and pulled a few sleeves – Bowie, *Diamond Dogs*, the Floyd, *Dark Side* and *Wish You Were Here*, and Dylan's *Blood on the Tracks*, an album that has never left me. What I would have given to listen to just one song. I hummed 'Tangled Up In Blue', a song I'd always marvelled over. I'd read entire novels that never came close to the truth and beauty of that song, and it ached my heart that I could never listen to it again.

There were also books in here. These I could still enjoy. I'd read often on the road, book after book. They were my one connection left to another human being. That's what books are – a direct link to another person's mind. They're a very private and personal magic. For they are magic, I can see that now. Human beings were storytellers above all else. It was our stock and trade for thousands upon thousands of years. Countless words all trying to explain what it meant to be human.

I guess we never figured it out.

But I suppose that's why I'm writing this down, because I am a human, the last human, still searching for answers, and because there's really nothing left to do.

From the dining room I moved upstairs to our room. There was the bed my wife and I slept in, talked in, argued in, made love in. Her clothes still hung in the wardrobe. I touched them, I smelled them, but my wife's scent was long gone. They were fusty and old, layered in filth and dust. There was a book by my side of the bed. The book I'd been reading before everything turned to shit. *David Copperfield*. My bookmark was still inside – page 153 to be exact. I figured it was time I finished the book.

From our bedroom I visited the bathroom and saw my wife in the bath, surrounded by candles on a night long ago. She was drinking champagne and laughing. The reality though was a bath yellowed and filthy. I pissed in my own toilet for the first time in four years, even though it couldn't be flushed, but I took pleasure in standing at my own bowl again, pissing, feeling, for one small moment, normal.

After this I crossed the landing and went into the back room, the final room. My boy's room.

This one hit me hardest. His bed looked small. So small. The covers, the curtains, the walls were like a shrine to the old mythologies of George Lucas and Stan Lee. I saw his toys and his clothes and realised after a time that I was crying. It had been a long time since I'd cried – Armageddon can make you numb after a while –

but it came in full force, shuddering through me. I went to my boy's window and looked down to our garden. It was overgrown, of course, but there was something that made me catch a gasp in my throat. Another face.

I stared at it. This face was made from the alignment of a fallen branch. I could make out a mouth, a crooked nose, hair, and two uneven eyes.

The face was looking right at me.

I opened the window.

"Afternoon," I said. "Nice day for it."

The face didn't look amused.

"You want hear something funny?"

The face didn't answer.

"I suppose it's funny peculiar, not funny ha-ha, but I've been thinking. I guess, in the end, we were only here for the blink of an eye. What would you say? Two-hundred thousand years? Three-hundred thousand? I heard them say that we didn't start migrating out of Africa until about fifty-thousand years ago. There were others, of course. Home erectus, Neanderthals, Denisovans, Heidelbergen-something or other – I heard those suckers lived about seven-hundred thousand years ago. Yet we were the only ones to evolve into intelligent beings... well, sorta intelligent. Seems like a bit of a misnomer now, don't it?

"Dinosaurs were here for about a hundred and fifty millions years. We didn't even make one million. We weren't even close. Big lizards did better than we did... and we were capable of so much... so much..."

A breeze kicked up and rustled through the trees. The sun remained fierce. I closed my eyes. I could almost hear an ice cream van in the distance and children out playing. I couldn't speak with the face any longer.

I closed the window and went back downstairs.

I busied myself skinning a rabbit I caught two days back. I used a couple of breezeblocks from the garage and spit the creature on my long knife, then I got a fire going. The face out front watched me as I went about my business and made small talk about this and that. Once the rabbit was nice and tender, I remembered the wine I had down in my cellar, and so I went down there to see if there were any left. There were ten bottles of red and three white. The cellar smelt damp. My son's first bike was down there, but I couldn't bring myself to look at it.

I returned to the kitchen and found a wine glass, then went through the garage again and picked up a fold-out chair.

I sat like a king in front of my house, stripping off rabbit flesh and drinking my wine. By now, the sun was low, spreading a golden haze over everything. I felt tired, so tired, but I enjoyed the wine, even though it made me sad. But it was a beautiful sadness. The-last-man-at-the-end-of-the-world-drinking-wine kind of sadness. The sun made everything beautiful, and utterly dreadful. I raised my glass to the smiling face at the front window. He didn't say anything but he appeared to appreciate the gesture.

I finished the whole bottle and then went up to my bed. The last embers of light lingered in the sky and a scattering of stars had begun their dance. I lay in bed and looked at the sky through my bedroom window as I had done so many times before. The bed covers smelt, but I didn't care. I was in my bed again, after all this time.

I tried to read some of *David Copperfield* by candlelight, but I couldn't concentrate and soon settled down into my pillow. Before I fell asleep I reached out for my wife's hand.

The next day I got busy. I rearranged furniture and moved ornaments and dressed curtains and tablecloths and clothes and toys and anything else I could find into a house full of faces. Some only worked if you were stood in a certain place, some worked the entire room. There was a face drawn onto the mirror in the bathroom, another made from piles of clothes out on the landing. There was one in the kitchen made from glasses and crockery. One on the banister made from coat hangers and old socks.

I spent most of the day creating the house of faces, then at dusk I skinned another rabbit and opened another bottle of wine. I felt tired, but content. It felt good to have people to talk to again. Every room I went into there was someone else I could say hello to. And they were all friendly and chatty and easy, apart from the guy in the garden. He was hard work, but I was determined to rise above his bad attitude and be the better man.

I ate my rabbit and drank my wine and watched the sun bleed across the sky.

I said to the guy behind me, "I wonder if they'll ever come back?"

The face at the front window said nothing. I guess he didn't know.

"It wasn't like in the movies," I said. "In the movies, they were always landing on the White House lawn or befriending little kids or blowing up the Empire State building. They didn't even have a ship. We didn't even see them, for fuck sake. There was just…"

I turned to look at the face. He was smiling. I didn't think it was the time to be smiling.

"I don't know why I'm still here."

The face said nothing.

"Maybe that was their plan. Maybe they're coming back for me…"

I realised I was crying again. I'd certainly turned that emotion back on.

"We didn't stand a chance… All the world's humans, gone… in the blink of an eye. Taken… every last one of them. I guess it took a week or so for every human to be collected up, but in that time we'd damn near ripped ourselves apart anyway…"

I looked to the dying brim of light on the horizon. "Jesus," I said. "*He* never came…"

I finished off the wine.

The next morning I set a few traps around the neighbourhood. If I was lucky I'd get a fox or cat, maybe even a dog. Rabbits were plentiful though and cooked just right, they were nice and tender. The house seemed crowded so I stayed out walking for a long while. I kept looking to the sky. In the old world, I always looked down, but now... now I was always looking up. I guess I was waiting. Waiting for them to return and take me.

I wondered if my wife and son were still alive. I suppose that was another reason why I always looked up now. Because they were out there, somewhere.

Back at the house, I opened another bottle of wine. I tried to read Dickens out front, but I kept feeling their eyes upon me. In the late afternoon I went up in the attic and got down the photo albums. Most of the albums were made up of pictures from mine and my wife's childhoods. In the age just before the end, everything became digital and people rarely developed their pictures and put them in albums. Yet, when the end came, all those billions of images of the human race were lost forever, including most of the pictures of our son.

I went through the photo albums and drank wine and became increasingly aware of the judgement from those staying in my house.

I looked at Christmases and summers and holidays and weddings and Halloweens and christenings. I looked at myself as I once was, a skinny kid into *Star Wars* and riding my bike and playing down the weir with my mates. I looked at my wife as she was in girlhood, long before I even knew her, standing with her parents on an overcast English beach, building a snowman with her father, and laughing in a backyard in a school dress with a friend I did not know. I looked at my own parents. They looked strange in their youth, like people recognised from a dream. I looked at each and every face.

Then I came to a picture of my wife and I just after we first met. We looked so young, so full of hope, so full of love. We looked like we were dressed to go out – shirt and tie/long, flowery dress – but I no longer remembered where. I threw the album to the ground and stood up.

I turned to the house and screamed, "Will you shut up!"

All went quiet.

"Thank you," I said, enraged.

I looked to the guy at the front of the house. "And what you are fuckin' smilin' about? Eh?"

He said nothing.

"Oh, you're fuckin' quiet now, aren't ya!"

I stormed inside and went to my room. I drank my own piss and got in bed, shaking.

I ran fingers across my ribs and felt each bone. My front teeth felt loose.

I didn't sleep well that night.

The next day, the final day in my own house, the voices grew even louder. The faces grew even stranger. The voices *were* voices, but they were indecipherable, a crowd of murmurs. A hum of life. I caught only snatches of words and none of them were good. My guests were turning on me.

I went out to the traps and found two rabbits and a hedgehog. The day was another hot one, but overcast. Very humid. The sky felt heavy.

I returned to the house with my dinner and found the place to be eerily quiet. A crow squawked on a telephone wire. The silence reminded me that I now lived in a world emptied of human beings. The world belonged to the creatures again. Out on the road I was nearly picked off by two dogs. I had to club them to death. Birds of prey circled over me regularly, waiting on the off chance I would keel over and die. There wasn't much meat on my bones anymore, but to a bird, or a dog, or a cat, or a fox, I probably looked pretty tasty still.

I put the dead creatures in the garage, then went and stood on the drive, looking at my house, and at the smiling face at my window.

"Why are you so quiet all of a sudden?"

He didn't answer. He couldn't, he was made of curtains and dirt.

"I lost my wife and child in a stampede in the city. Hundreds... probably thousands of people all running, crushing, trampling... tearing at each other. I had my boy in my arms and my wife at my side, but then I was knocked to the ground and my boy went sprawling and was carried away on the wave of bodies. My wife went after him and that was the last time I ever saw them."

The crow squawked again.

"I went after them, of course, but the flow of people was too great. And then..."

I looked at the smiling face. "I don't know how you're still here," I said. "How did you escape? Did you see all those people in the sky... all those thousands of people? A rapture, I suppose..."

The face smiled at this.

"If I hadn't found the vault, I would have been taken too."

I shook my head and wiped my eyes. "I wish I had been..."

I went into the house and opened another bottle of wine, then I sat out front and drank the entire thing as dark thunderheads moved across the sky. The air smelt electric.

The wine worked its way into my system and distant thunder rumbled across the sky. Moments of epiphany come when you least expect it, and this one was no exception. It came on like the lightning that forked from land to sky. A wicked flash across my mind. I'd returned to the house to reclaim the past, but there was nothing to reclaim. It was a house of memories, a house of ghosts, slowly being taken over by interlopers. My past, my history, were now untenable.

Thunder boomed over the rooftops and the rain came on as if God had flicked on a switch. I didn't move.

I just sat, drinking my wine, thinking on how far away from human I now felt. I wondered how much longer I could last. I wondered how much longer I *should* last.

Another shock of lightning, another roll of thunder, closer now. The rain hissed as it hit the earth. I felt cold but continued drinking my wine. I raised the bottle to the sky and tilted it to my wife and child out there in the stars.

Finally, I got up and headed into the garage. I found the petrol can and then went inside. I dowsed the sofa, the curtains, the kitchen table. I didn't look at any of the faces. I dowsed the banister, my bed, my wife's clothes, my son's bed. I went back downstairs and rifled in a draw for a box of matches. They were where I'd left them.

I went and stood out on the threshold. Thunder boomed overhead and I lit a match. I threw it in and stood back.

I waltzed around as the building burned. Another Bob Dylan line, but I did it. I burned my past, my history, my loves and I danced in the storm. I burned all that was left of me. I burned away the last of my humanity. It was the only way I could survive.

Hard rain, dark sky, black smoke, blood flames. It took it away, every last drop of me.

After a while I lay out on the road. The thunder moved off and the rain abated. The sky remained dark and my house roared.

I noticed a mangy dog watching me from across the way. I saw his hungry eyes, his panting tongue. I growled at him and he fled. I decided that I would no longer speak words, only write them. The last vestige of what I once was.

At one point, I thought I heard screams coming from the house, but I couldn't be sure.

At one point, I thought I heard my wife calling me, but I couldn't be sure.

At one point, I thought I saw a plane crossing the black sky, but I couldn't be sure.

WHAT YOU SEE IS
WHAT YOU GET

The Contributors

❊

G.V. ANDERSON is a World Fantasy Award-winning writer whose stories have appeared in *Strange Horizons, Fantasy & Science Fiction, Lightspeed*, and *Nightmare*.

~

ANDREW DAVID BARKER was born in Derby, England in 1975. He is an author and filmmaker. His first novel, *The Electric*, was released in 2013 to critical acclaim: a movie version is currently in development. As a filmmaker, he wrote and directed the cult, post-apocalyptic indie feature, *A Reckoning*, in 2011, and has recently made the award-winning short films, *Two Old Boys* and *Shining Tor*, and scripted the Sci-Fi short, *Endling*. He is also the author of the video nasty era, coming of age novella, *Dead Leaves*, and the short ghost story collection, *Winter Freits*. He lives in Warwickshire with his wife and daughter, trying to be a grown up.

~

CHARLOTTE BOND is an author, ghostwriter, freelance editor, proofreader, reviewer, and podcaster. Under her own name, she has written within the genres of horror and dark fantasy. As a ghostwriter, she's tackled everything from romance to cozy mystery stories and YA novels. She is a reviewer for the Ginger Nuts of Horror website, as well as the British Fantasy Society and the Jane and Bex Book Blog. Her articles have appeared in such places as Tor.com, War History Online, The Vintage News, and Writing Magazine. She is a co-host of the podcast *Breaking the Glass Slipper*, which in 2018 was shortlisted for a BFS award for best audio and was longlisted for a Hugo.

~

DANIEL BRAUM is the American author of the short story collections *The Night Marchers and Other Strange Tales* (Cemetery Dance 2016), *The Wish Mechanics: Stories of the Strange and Fantastic* (Independent Legions 2017) and the chapbook *Yeti Tiger Dragon Leopard* (Dim Shores 2016). His third collection, *Underworld Dreams* is forthcoming from Lethe Press. His first novel, *The Serpent's Shadow*, is forthcoming from Cemetery Dance. He is the editor of *Spirits Unwrapped* from Lethe Press and host and founder of the *Night Time Logic* reading series in New York City. He can be found at **facebook.com/DanielBraumFiction** and **bloodandstardust.wordpress.com**.

~

ELIZA CHAN writes about East Asian mythology, British folklore and madwomen in the attic, but preferably all three at once. She likes to collect folk tales and modernise them with a twist of lemon, pinch of pepper and a kilo of surrealism. Her work has been published in *Podcastle*, British Fantasy Award nominated *Asian Monsters* and *Fantasy Magazine*. She is currently working on a fantasy novel about waterdragons and a flooded world. You can find her on twitter **@elizawchan** or her website **elizawchan.wordpress.com**

RICH HAWKINS hails from the depths of Somerset, England, where a childhood of science fiction and horror films set him on the path to writing his own stories. He credits his love of horror and all things weird to his first viewing of John Carpenter's *The Thing* back in the early Nineties. His debut novel *The Last Plague* was nominated for a British Fantasy Award for Best Horror Novel in 2015. His forthcoming works include the apocalyptic novel *The Cold* from Horrific Tales Publishing.

~

CARLY HOLMES lives and writes in an estuary village on the banks of the river Teifi in west Wales. Her award-winning short fiction has been published in numerous anthologies and journals and her debut novel, *The Scrapbook*, was shortlisted for the International Rubery Book Award in 2015. *Figurehead*, her Literary Strange short story collection, was published by Tartarus Press in 2018. Carly works as an editor and marketing officer with Parthian Books, and spends her free time worrying.

~

TIM MAJOR's love of speculative fiction is the product of a childhood diet of classic Doctor Who episodes and an early encounter with Triffids. Tim's most recent books are SF thriller *Snakeskins* and a short story collection, *And the House Lights Dim* – others include *Machineries of Mercy*, *You Don't Belong Here* and a non-fiction book about the 1915 silent crime film, *Les Vampires*. His short stories have appeared in *Interzone* and *Not One of Us* and have been selected for *Best of British Science Fiction* and *The Best Horror of the Year*. **cosycatastrophes.com**

ROSANNE RABINOWITZ lives in South London where she engages in several occupations including care work and freelance editing. Her novella, *Helen's Story*, was shortlisted for the 2013 Shirley Jackson Award, and her stories have appeared in various anthologies. Her first collection, *Resonance & Revolt*, was published by Eibonvale Press in 2018. She spends a lot of time drinking coffee – or whisky – and listening to loud music while looking out of her tenth-floor window.

~

SARAH READ is a dark fiction writer in the frozen north of Wisconsin. Her short stories can be found in Gamut, Black Static, and other places, and in various anthologies including *Suspended in Dusk, BEHOLD! Oddities Curiosities and Undefinable Wonders* and *The Best Horror of the Year Vol 10*. Her novel *The Bone Weaver's Orchard* is now out from Trepidatio Publishing, and her debut collection *Out of Water* will follow in November 2019. She is the Editor-in-Chief of *Pantheon* Magazine and of their associated anthologies, including *Gorgon: Stories of Emergence*. She is an active member of the Horror Writers Association. When she's not staring into the abyss, she knits. Keep up with her at her website, **inkwellmonsterwordpress.com**, or follow her on Twitter or Instagram **@Inkwellmonster**.

❋ ❋ ❋

JAMES EVERINGTON mainly writes dark, supernatural fiction, although he occasionally takes a break and writes dark, non-supernatural fiction. His second collection of such tales, *Falling Over*, is out now from Infinity Plus. He's also the author of *The Quarantined City*, an episodic novel mixing Borgesian strangeness with supernatural horror – *"an unsettling voice all of its own"* The Guardian – the novellas *Paupers' Graves* and *The Shelter*, and the mini-collection *Trying To Be So Quiet & Other Hauntings*. Oh, and he drinks Guinness, if anyone's asking. You can find out what James is currently up to at his website, **jameseverington.blogspot.co.uk**.

~

DAN HOWARTH is a Mancunian born writer and editor who is now living on Merseyside and experiencing true horror first hand. Dan's short fiction has been published in a variety of places, including *No Monsters Allowed* (edited by Alex Davis), *The Hyde Hotel*, *Stories of the Dead: A Tribute to George A. Romero* and as a stand-alone title *Dulce Et Decorum Est* from Demain Publishing. Like all Northerners he enjoys pies, rain and drinking blood from the skulls of his enemies. Dan can be tracked down to his website, **danhowarthwriter.com**, which features news of his writing and book reviews.

~

Together, James and Dan have co-edited the anthologies *The Hyde Hotel* (Black Shuck Books) and the BFS Award-nominated *Imposter Syndrome* (Dark Minds Press).

❋ ❋ ❋